DAN DARE

PILOT OF THE FUTURE

*Other books in this series available from New English Library:*

NO TEARS FOR MOLLY by June Vincent
ROY OF THE ROVERS by James Hart
D-DAY DAWSON by Marcus Allgood

# DAN DARE

## PILOT OF THE FUTURE

FRANK HAMPSON

NEW ENGLISH LIBRARY
TIMES MIRROR

A New English Library Original Publication 1977


*

FIRST NEL PAPERBACK EDITION MAY 1977

*



*NEL Books are published by*
*New English Library Limited from Barnard's Inn, Holborn, London EC1N 2JR.*
*Made and printed in Great Britain by Hunt Barnard Printing Ltd., Aylesbury, Bucks.*

45003320 I

## CHAPTER ONE

# HELLO, VENUS – GOODBYE!

Melted beyond endurance, the permanon-steel lattice-work of the launch gantry tumbled away like so much spaghetti as *Kingfisher*, like a giant aluminium cucumber, lifted slowly away on its blazing tail-jets, the glaring fire from its belly dazzlingly white, even through the polarised glass of the stressed windows in the command observation bunker. The concrete of the apron shimmered in the backlash of the huge engines, and Sir Hubert Guest felt the harsh edges of the control console vibrate beneath his clutching fingers, cutting so sharply into his hands that he had to let go and, assuming his customary pose of calm and quiet, fold his arms.

'Well, she's off, Dan.' He turned, smiling with an expression that he knew to be false, to the slim, tall, dark-eyed man by his side. A man whose strangely arched eyebrows lifted just a little. Just enough to show that he, at least, saw through the put-on complacency of the Chief Controller of the Interplanetary Space Fleet.

'We don't know exactly what destroyed *Orion* and *Argonaut*, sir.' Dan Dare's hands made to rise in a throwaway gesture, but he controlled them, thrusting them suddenly into his pockets. Sir Hubert looked away, aware now that they were both putting

on an act. That both of them knew how desperately important this mission of the spacecraft *Kingfisher* really was. That both of them knew it might end in disaster, as had the previous shots to investigate the distant planet Venus . . .

'Look, don't worry, Sir Hubert.' Dan Dare had decided not to play games with his commander. Colonel of the space fleet, he had been anxious that he himself would command the *Kingfisher* mission. But he'd been overruled. Too important to risk. Now he said: '*Orion* and *Argonaut* were proved to have faults, sir. We found them on the drawing board. Too late, unhappily . . . ' Dan bit his lip. 'But then,' he continued, 'they actually got within range of Venus! They were almost *there*, sir . . . before engine fatigue, or whatever, did for them!'

'Yes, Dan. Did for them. They exploded. And they were up there on my orders. I don't mind telling you – it makes me feel like a murderer.'

Dan Dare's hand closed over the older man's arm. 'You mustn't think like that, sir! Exploration of space is *bound* to involve risks! You did everything you could, in line with available knowledge! Nobody could have done any more!'

'I know, Dan. I know. But I'm worried. Worried that our modifications – our adjustments – haven't done enough for *Kingfisher*. If that craft comes to grief, I'm broken. Absolutely broken.'

Flung bodily from the launch-pad by the thrust of its initial engines, *Kingfisher* lanced like an arrow up into the blue, the flare from its tail visible to the watchers for no more than a brief instant. Then it was gone – curving through the ever-darkening layers of the earth's atmosphere, the vague clouds of its home already merging with the gentle curve of the planet's surface way, way behind. At the controls, Captain Crane unstrapped himself and turned to the three members of his crew.

'Johnny. We're clear. Tell 'em so. Dick. Run over the dials and make sure none of our cargo's shifted, will you?'

His experienced eye checked that the auto-pilot was functioning. Until they'd passed the pull of the moon, they wouldn't have to check and re-correct. 'I'm for some grub – while we've still got internal pressure enough to eat it without squeezing it out of tubes. Anyone else?'

'Roger, skipper!' Dick Vanbrugh turned from his bank of equipment and raised his thumb. 'I got Nancy to part up with the stuff she'd prepared for Colonel Dare. She made 'em good. She thought *he* was coming on this mission!'

'So did Colonel Dare.' Crane laughed. 'Darned shame. A pilot like him – been stuck in a chair for lord knows how long. Bit of a flap, and he reckons he'll be back behind the controls. Oh well – I suppose it's a bit of a toss-up who's going to be the first on Venus.'

Johnny Walters, co-pilot, turned to his captain, having carried out his orders. 'Do you really reckon we'll find what we want there, sir?'

'I reckon. Massive cloud cover, sure. And no real telling what's below it. But probes have informed us that there *is* soil – and in parts, atmosphere in which we can grow crops. That's the whole thing, Johnny – crops. We're living on an earth that's becoming so rapidly over-populated that food's a vital concern. So many people, so little space! We've got to find an area that can support us, and the moon's no good . . .'

'Neither's Mars,' said Dick Vanbrugh, laconically. 'We know what happened to the ships that went *there*! Nothing but sand and heat! Plenty of vitamin D in a sun-tan, but that doesn't keep a man alive!'

'As you say, Dick.' Captain Crane made a slight adjustment to the controls as a green light flickered briefly on the panel. 'But Venus, now – that's something else. Why, if we're to believe what we've been told, there are all kinds of life-supporting vegetation already growing there!'

Johnny frowned. Looked down at his hands. He said, 'Captain. Doesn't it strike you that if there are such things on Venus, there might be people too? People who'd resent us coming to – sort of – poach . . . ?'

Time had passed. A lot of time, for Dan Dare. Still irritated that he had been passed over for command of the *Kingfisher* mission, he had fretted and fumed over desk-bound papers and day-to-day work, scanning files, initialling them, flinging them into his out-tray. Feeling that a Colonel's job shouldn't have to be so tied to routine. He'd snarled at his secretary, cursed the commissionaire, damned his batman to here and beyond! But that batman, the redoubtable Digby, had remained totally unmoved, and now, seven days after the launch of *Kingfisher*, he brought Dan Dare's breakfast with the same dignified aplomb that he always used. As he'd said to himself just before he opened the door of Dan's room, glancing at himself in the mirror, 'Nay, then – he's a reet tartar at some times, but Colonel Dare can't be perfect! After all, he's not a Lancashire lad like me!'

'Morning, Dig,' Dan Dare's greeting was just friendly. 'Bacon and eggs?'

'Nobbut them vitamin blocks, sir,' said Digby.

'Jumpin' jets!' Dan blew up, but Digby didn't even flinch. He was used to it! 'If I eat much more of these things I'll begin to *look* like a flaming vitamin!'

'You're frettin', sir,' said Digby, fussing round his chief. 'I dunno why you keep angry about not goin' on *Kingfisher*! Me – I'm glad. I don't want to go gaddin' about to nasty planets like Mars . . . '

'It's Venus, Digby . . . '

'Well, Venus! What's the difference? I tell thee, sir, there's nowt like Wigan! A man could be happy in a spot like that!'

Dan laughed, picked up the plate of synthetic food, and hurled it into his waste-bin. 'I don't know what they eat in

Wigan, Dig, but it certainly isn't this! Forget orders, and get me some proper scoff! *And* you can cook some for yourself, if you want!'

'I already have, sir. I'll serve it you, and I'll make some more.' Digby vanished back into the kitchen.

It was at that moment that the telephone – the red telephone that connected Dan directly with his headquarters – shrilled urgently. The voice on the other end was Sir Hubert's, and the problem was *Kingfisher*!

'Dig!' Dan bellowed as he slammed down the phone. 'Never mind breakfast! We're going to HQ – pronto! There's trouble – *big* trouble!'

'*Kingfisher* bearing ZN 76 – AL 34!' The tracking operator's voice in Space Fleet headquarters was unnaturally shrill. 'Cross bearing from the moon XC51 – NT 178! We've got her in the viewer, sir!'

Dan shook his mind clear of the confusion of the ops room and turned to Sir Hubert Guest. 'What *is* this, Sir Hubert?'

'Bad news, Dan. *Kingfisher*'s entered the area where *Orion* and *Argonaut* blew up! And radio contact's gone haywire. We can just about hear them, but they're not reading us at all. There's some kind of ray affecting them. The same sort of thing that cut out the others. This time, we can monitor it, but it seems *Kingfisher*, despite her modifications, is in real trouble!'

RIGHT—KINGFISHER WAS POWERED WITH IMPULSE WAVE ENGINES WASN'T SHE?

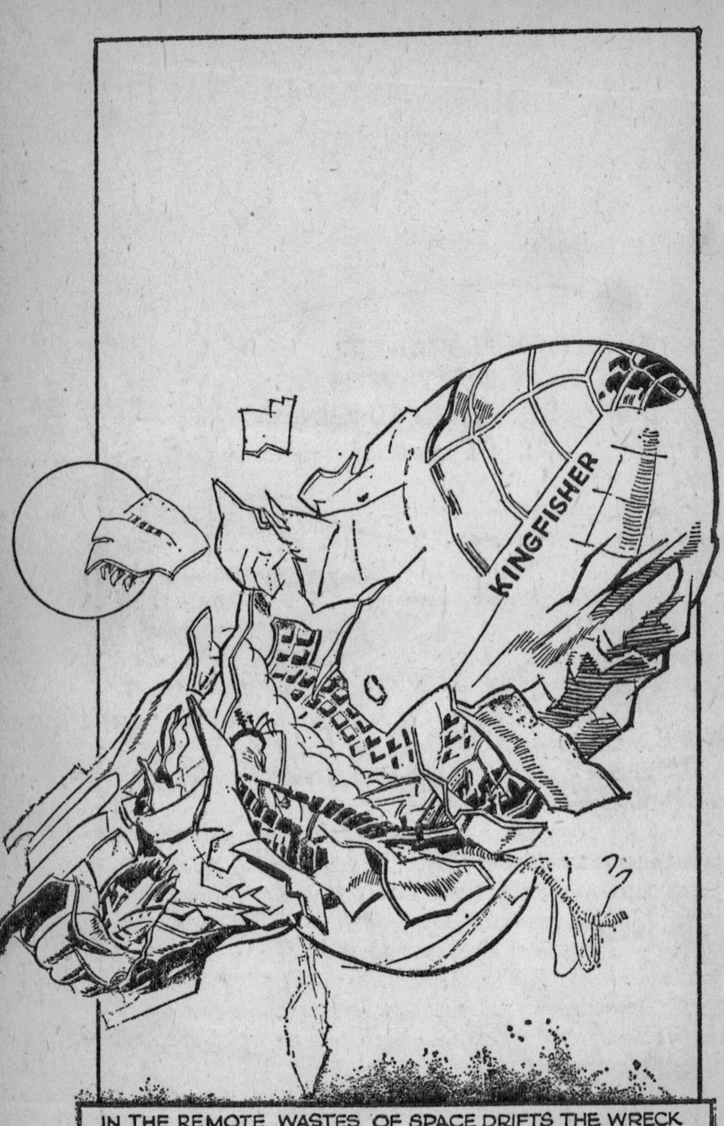
KINGFISHER
IN THE REMOTE WASTES OF SPACE DRIFTS THE WRECK OF THE "KINGFISHER" BLOWN APART IN THE LATEST ATTEMPT TO REACH VENUS, THE MYSTERY PLANET.

'Come in, *Kingfisher*! Captain Crane – come *in*!' Dan's fists clenched. He looked at Digby but found no reassurance in the round, open face.

'Do you copy, *Kingfisher*? Over!'

The speeding spaceship sped onwards towards Venus, its impulse motors – which drew energy from signals beamed from Earth – at full stretch. It was no more than an hour away from the mysterious planet. And although he knew there were communications difficulties with Earth, Captain Crane was unworried.

But then came the report from the engine area. The sudden, frantic report!

'The impulse cylinders, sir! They – they're breaking up!'

'Whaaat? Stop jets! Close five, seven and eight bulkheads! Break out oxygen and pressure suits!' Crane saw the intercommunications box leap from the desk in front of him even as he shouted the words. Knew then that it was too late! The last thing his eyes registered was the undulating bulge of the very fabric of *Kingfisher*! The palpitating shudder of the pressure-walls before his face in the fractional instant before the whole craft blew apart with an almighty, devastating explosion.

Where *Kingfisher* had been, there was nothing but a drifting whirl of space-dust.

CHAPTER TWO

## TRY, TRY, TRY AGAIN!

It was cold. So very cold. Digby pulled his jacket closer round his ample frame and shuddered. This wasn't like Wigan! This was like nothing on earth, and besides, he'd never wanted to leave earth anyway, not when he'd volunteered for the Spaceforce! He heard himself whimpering . . . 'Cook! Storeman! Clerk! That's what I wanted to be – with a nice uniform to go on leave with, and impress them Lancashire lasses! Why did I have to go and end up batman to a bloke who dumps me on Mercury, freezing in an over-compensated suit while the temperature outside's enough to fry bacon butties in half a second flat . . . ?'

Then the torrid surface of the sun's nearest neighbour seemed to fade away, and – as if from afar, Digby heard the call of his Colonel.

'Digby! Dig-*beee*!'

'Nnuhhh? Wha . . . ? Lumme, I was dreamin'!'

'You certainly were, you daft ha'porth! Now stir your stumps and get out of that Jepeet!'

Digby blinked is eyes once or twice. No Colonel Dan in vision. The voice must be coming through the radio . . .

'Digby! Can you *hear* me, you Lancashire hot-pot?'

'Eee, I'm awake now, sir!' Dig pulled the microphone from

its retaining clips on the dash of the personal jet-propelled gyroscopic jeep – the 'Jepeet' that was Dan Dare's own vehicle.

'Get out of there and bring a helicar to headquarters roof! You've got to pick up the controller and myself. And quickly!'

Digby did as he was told. Once alert, the fat man from the North could move faster than the casual observer might think! Within three minutes, the rotors of a helicar were in smooth neutral while Dan Dare and Sir Hubert Guest climbed aboard.

'Where are we going, sir?'

'To an emergency meeting of the cabinet, Dig. *Kingfisher*'s loss has put the whole lot in a panic, and they're determined to cancel the whole Venus project!'

'So they should, Colonel Dan.' Digby spun the controls deftly and whipped the car round the spire of a church – a relic of the London of the past.

'No, Dig! You're wrong! Just because we've lost three missions, it doesn't mean the quest is hopeless! You see – all the spacecraft's we've used were powered by impulse-wave engines!'

'Sorry, sir. I don't get it.'

'Neither did I, Digby, when Colonel Dare first expounded his theory!' Sir Hubert Guest leaned forward eagerly and Digby, without looking round, could sense the excitement in the Controller.

'Suppose – just suppose there's a hostile element on Venus. Beings who've put up a *force-field* at the limits of their atmos-

phere! Remember the last words we heard from *Kingfisher*? Something about "the impulse cylinders"! Think what would happen if a ship, carrying a huge load of impulse waves in those cylinders, hit a force-field . . . '

Casually, for although his mind was on Sir Hubert's words, his reactions were steady, Digby put his left hand down and squeezed the helicar through the twin towers of Westminster Abbey, heading for the landing pad on the House of Parliament.

'By 'eck, you're right! I *know* what'd happen . . . . !'

'Just so, Dig!' Dan Dare tapped his finger on the back of the seat. 'What'd happen would be *exactly* what happened to *Kingfisher*! A total explosion!'

Digby brought the craft smoothly round over the wide expanse of the new recreation areas that had replaced old Victoria and Saint James's, and requested permission to land from the ever-watchful cabinet police. He said, 'So we can't get near the planet, sir?'

'Wrong, Dig,' grinned Dan Dare. 'Touch down and wait! I've got a feeling you're going to be seeing more than you ever dreamed of when you stepped out of your Wigan front door . . . and you're going to see it fairly shortly!'

'Oh, 'eck! If it's all the same to you, I'd rather not, sir!'

This time, while he waited, Digby didn't sleep. He was too worried. And the expression on Dan Dare's face when he and Sir Hubert Guest returned did nothing to reassure him.

'We've got the go-ahead, Digby,' said Dare. 'They're getting

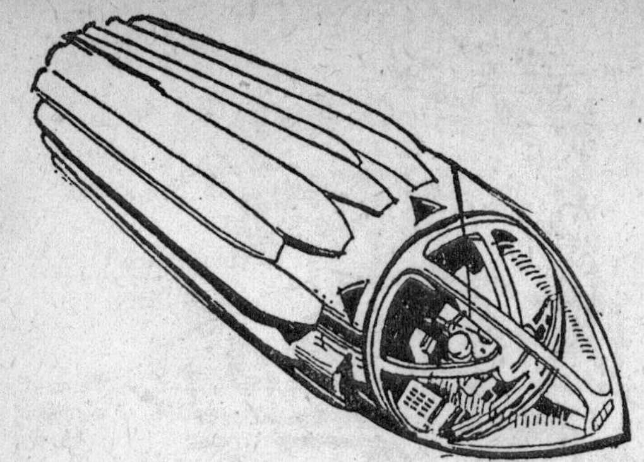

our new ship ready as from now!'

'Ship? Now look 'ere, Colonel Dan – we're not going galavanting off to Venus, surely? Not with that there force-field, an' all . . . ?'

'The ship's going to take us *almost* there, Dig. Almost, but not quite. Okay – she'll be powered by impulse wave engines, just like *Kingfisher*, but she'll pull up before she gets within range of their defences . . .'

'An' then we sit tight an' take pictures?'

'We do *not*, Digby! We transfer to self-contained rocket ferries, carrying their own fuel. They'll take us safely through the danger zone!'

Digby let in the controls of the helicar and moaned loudly. An act, of course – for wherever his Colonel Dan went, the tubby Lancastrian would always go. But he had to say it. 'You'll be the death of me, sir! The very death!'

'I hope not, Digby.' Now it was Sir Hubert Guest, his voice deceptively level. 'Colonel Dare will be picking up a special crew for this mission, but the fact is, *I'm* going, too.'

'*You*, Sir Hubert?' Digby couldn't keep the surprise out of his voice.

'Me. Everything is being staked on this project. And everything includes me!'

'Eh, well. It includes me, an' all,' said Digby, and flew on . . .

It couldn't happen immediately. The governmental processes, the okays for this and that programme had to be thrashed out.

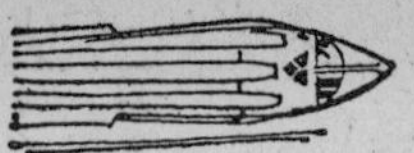

But incredibly – or maybe not so incredibly, since the world leader knew that a new food-base was so totally necessary – the new Venus ship was built in a mere three months. Built, along with its ancillary rockets – the small vehicles to carry earthmen through to Venus despite the force-field.

It was in one such of the ancillary rockets that Dan Dare flew, on a test flight, to the military airfield, at Prairie-du-Lac, Canada. Both to try out the machine and to pick up the rest of his crew. With him went Digby and Sir Hubert . . .

'Now what in heck d'you reckon *that* contraption is, Pierre?' Hank Hogan, tall, lean and bespectacled, dressed like the dumpy man beside him in the green uniform of the Interplanetary Space Fleet, shaded his eyes and frowned. Pierre Lafayette spread his hands and shrugged expressively. 'She looks like a rocket ship to me, Hank.'

'She's landing here,' muttered the tall American. 'You're right, Pierre – she *is* a rocket. What have we joined now – a museum?'

The rocketship made a roaring pass over the field at Prairie-du-Lac and turned neatly, her nose dropping as she came in to land. 'I suppose,' said Hank, 'we've got the right place?' Pierre nodded. 'Dan's telegram said landing area X–1, and this *is* it!'

Then, as the rocket coasted towards them on its triple undercart and rolled to a halt, the eyes of the two friends opened wide in disbelief! The side door slid open, and . . .

'For Pete's sake! *Dan*! What in thunder are you doing in *that* thing?'

'Hello, Hank. Pierre.' Dan Dare extended his hand for the pair of warm, friendly shakes and grinned at his old comrades. 'It's good to see you both again.'

'Certainement, mon ami! But answer Hank's question, Dan! Why ze veteran transport?'

'She's no veteran, Pierre. Brand new. Don't you like her?' Dan paused. 'You'd better get used to her, boys – you're going to fly one of her sisters in the next attempt on Venus!'

Hank gasped. Laughed at what he fondly imagined to be a joke. Then reddened as he realised Dan was in deadly earnest! '*Venus*? So that's it! A suicide club! Well, you can elect *me* out!'

'No suicide at all, Hank. Come into the mess, both of you, and Sir Hubert and I will give you the gen.' Hank and Pierre gulped, saluted the figure of Sir Hubert, who'd stepped down to join them, and followed their Colonel towards the airfield main buildings. At a properly respectful distance, Spaceman Albert Fitz-William Digby trailed along behind . . .

It didn't take Dan long to outline the plan. He summarised. 'You see, our little rocket kites will be carried by a big ship, rather like planes on an old aircraft carrier. We make our lone take-off when we're near the force-field danger zone. If my theory is right, we'll sail clear through to Venus.'

'Yeah, *if* you're right,' said Hank, gloomily.

'How many will be going on zis trip, Dan?' Now it was Pierre who spoke, tugging thoughtfully at the short moustache on his upper lip.

'Six of us. You two, Sir Hubert, Digby, myself, and Professor Peabody.'

'Professor Peabody? Who's he?' The French-Canadian looked blank, and in return, Dan looked even blanker! 'We don't know. Some old greybeard, I suppose. The cabinet are sending him to check the full possibilities of growing food on Venus.'

At that moment, there was a tap on the door, and Digby came in. He coughed for their attention. 'Er – Professor Peabody, sir . . . '

Dan, Sir Hubert, Hank and Pierre rose to greet 'the old greybeard'. But their polite mutters of greeting died in their throats! To a man, they stood riveted, their eyes incredulously registering the tall, slim figure who swept in past the grinning Digby. For the professor was not at all the sort of person any of them had expected!

'Jumpin' jets! It – it's a *woman*!'

Professor Jocelyn Peabody sat down, crossed her slender legs and swept them all with a somewhat chilly glance!

It was crystal clear that Professor Peabody had no doubts of her equality as a female with these seasoned spacemen! It was equally clear that Sir Hubert Guest had no intention whatever of taking what he called 'a mere female' along on the mission! Instantly, he put a call through the cabinet headquarters – and received a direct snub for his pains! 'I'm afraid you must take her, Sir Hubert,' said the anonymous voice at the other end. 'It's a direct and irrevocable order from the cabinet!'

Sir Hubert slammed down the receiver. He said 'Pah!'. He opened his mouth as if to say even more, thought better of it, and slammed out of the room!

'Welcome, anyway, Professor,' smiled Dan. 'We're going to serve together, so there's no sense in starting off on the wrong foot. Sir Hubert won't be long in accepting fate, I promise!' The girl laughed. 'Don't worry – I'm used to this sort of thing, Colonel Dare. One of the hazards of my job!'

It was one week later. The three rocketships had been mounted on to the huge spacecraft *Ranger*, and now the friends had gathered to join the mother ship for the fourth attempt on the mystery planet.

'Any more for the *Skylark*? Get your tickets here! Returns only!' Pierre chuckled at Hank's ever-present good humour.

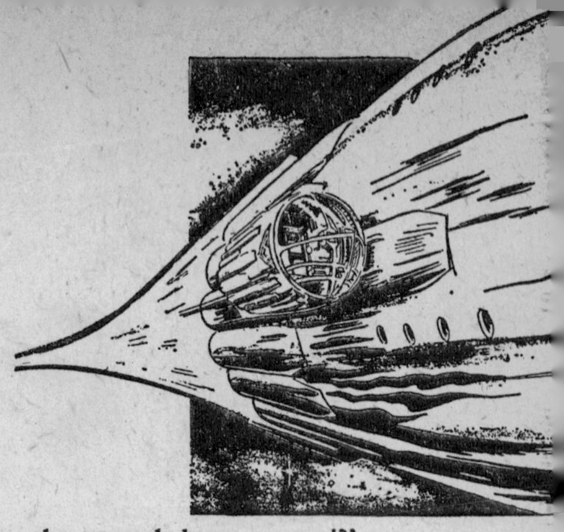

'Suppose we don't use the return halves, mon ami?'

'You get your money back,' said Dan, evenly.

The lift-off and running of *Ranger* was no concern of Dan and his friends. Until they entered their own rocketships, they were no more than passengers. On the bridge of the big mother ship, Captain Hunter gave the orders that started up the massive jets. Gently, the pivoted launch ramp raised the impulse-powered giant through eighty-five degrees, almost to the vertical.

'Check shock-straps! Check ignition monitors! Check gantry release . . . ' One by one, the complex procedures were put into operation. Then – 'Ready to launch!'

With a surging blast of power, *Ranger* stood inert for a seemingly endless moment and then, so swiftly that the human eye couldn't follow, accelerated away from the apron. Away from the tense watchers in the command blockhouse. Away from planet Earth on the first stage of its vital journey. There could be no second thoughts. No change of plans. Not now . . .

CHAPTER THREE

## BREAK-UP!

The globe of Earth dwindled steadily behind the hurtling spaceship until it became no more than a far-off speck in the spangled sky. And now, as automatic ranging devices zeroed the craft on its voyage, the planet Venus became the focus of attention, both for Captain Hunter and his crew, and for Dan and his exploration force.

Mere time, in the absence of any sensation of night or day, had little meaning. But at last, the order so long awaited came through the intercom from the command area. 'Rocketship crews stand by for launching! Suit up, please!'

Digby mournfully stared down at the jigsaw he'd failed to complete, and hoped desperately that he might have time to finish it another day! Muttering to himself, he got into the bulky pressure suit and stood for Dan's inspection, helmet in his hand. 'Do I look right, sir?'

Dan laughed. There was an enormous bulge at Digby's midriff – a built-in parachute system. 'That waistchute doesn't help your figure, Dig – but I think you'll do!'

The three teams checked their equipment and entered their rockets. They felt the mothership check as the impulse motors

were cut. Then all was steady as gyro stabilisers came into play.

'Number Two ship – Dare and Digby – ready.' Dan flicked over the switch of his radio.

'Number Three ship – Lafayette and Hogan – ready.'

There was no crackling message from Number One. Digby glanced at his colonel, wryly. 'Fancy Sir Hubert taking the Prof in his rocket, sir – after the way he's been carrying on about her!'

Dan smiled. 'He said he wants to keep his eye on her, Dig. Make sure she doesn't get in the way!' He chuckled. 'I imagine there's a bit of an argument going on already!'

Dan was right! Sir Hubert, fuming helplessly, was trying to order Jocelyn Peabody away from Number One rocket's controls. 'I insist you let me handle this craft! Do you hear me?'

Professor Peabody shook her head. 'Sorry, Sir Hubert. You're not as young as you used to be – and we may need steady nerves on this job!'

Sir Hubert spluttered furiously. Words just wouldn't come! And then it was too late. With a crisp 'okay' to *Ranger*'s commander, the girl thrust forward the release lever and gunned the rocket engines that shot the little craft into space. 'We're off!'

With Numbers Two and Three trailing their port and starboard quarters, Number One hurtled through the void towards the ever-larger planet. Sir Hubert had grumpily succumbed to his companion's undoubtedly strong will-power! 'Very well, Miss Peabody. You will pilot this vessel. However, I may decide to charge you with insubordination when we reach Venus!'

'*If* we reach Venus,' replied the girl, her matter-of-fact voice making her superior gnash his teeth with fresh rage and frustration. How could this – this woman be so damnably *cool* . . . ?

Now they were running hard for target, and Dan's instruments showed that they were nearing the danger area. The area where *Orien*, *Argonaut* and *Kingfisher* had met their doom. The colonel heard Sir Hubert's testy voice in his radiophones. 'Ships Two and Three cut engines. You too, Miss Peabody.'

They hung poised above the great globe of the planet, and Sir Hubert's voice came through again. More controlled, now . . .

'Righto, Dig?' Dan Dare turned to his rather white-faced companion. 'So we go in first. Just cross all your fingers and hang on to your hat!'

The nose of the little space vehicle lanced down into the belt of treacherous rays – the killing force-field. There was slight vibration – no more! 'I think we might *make* it, Digby!'

Digby's voice was like a croak, but his complexion had recovered all its colour. 'You must've been right about the rays only attacking impulse motors, sir! Rockets *are* the answer!'

But then it happened! Without warning, the whole structure of the rocketship's radio equipment blew apart with a shattering

explosion, and the cabin filled with acrid smoke!

Somehow, Dan Dare held the plunging ship on course. 'What *idiots* we were! The *radio's* worked by impulse waves!'

Digby came spluttering up to his colonel. 'It caught fire, sir – but I put it out with an extinguisher! Trouble is, the plates are badly strained on the starboard side!'

Dan said, grimly, 'They might not hold out, Digby. And if they give way . . . '

Digby closed his eyes and thought of good old Wigan. He'd have given a fortune to be there now. But he wasn't. He was on a frail bit of man-made junk, belting down towards goodness-only-knew what and threatening to break up at any moment! The vibration began . . . and built. Until he was suddenly aware of a new light glowing on the control panel beside him!

'Colonel Dan, sir! The atmosphere light's on! We've hit the air round Venus! We've *done* it!'

Any watcher below would have seen the ship come arrowing down through the thick atmosphere. Would have seen fire break out all over its structure as Dan Dare fought to keep it in one piece. And then, even as it began to level out, such a watcher would have seen the white billow of twin parachutes as the two friends jettisoned themselves clear!

And they were only just in time! Hanging from his harness, his portly batman already blown well clear of him, Dan saw the rocketship turn over in the instant before it blew itself to smithereens! Rocked by the blast, Dan's senses reeled. A

momentary blackout! And then he saw himself dropping swiftly towards the surface of a wave-chopped sea!

'Time to get rid of the 'chute! Thank the stars for this quick release gadget!' Dan punched the button, and a split-second later fell headlong into the drink!

Down, down, down . . . aware of the bubbles streaming past him. Automatically holding his breath until he realised that his own helmet and pressure-suit, with its built-in breathing apparatus, would keep him safe.

Dan had time to register that there was life here on Venus. Strange, multi-coloured fish swam into his vision and out again – seemingly unafraid. Then he was rising again, and his last picture of Digby flashed into his mind. 'He was dropping well to my right . . . towards some crags! I hope the fat chump had the sense to manoeuvre away from them . . .'

He broke surface and began to swim strongly towards the distant, rocky shore. But all at once, he was conscious of a turbulance in the water ahead. He eased his strokes, cautiously. Then gasped with horror as a huge scaly head shattered the sea like a smashed mirror! The rearing, awsome head of a ferocious, glaring beast more frightening than anything that might once have stalked the prehistoric Earth!

High above Venus, ships One and Three were still hovering. Pierre came over the intercom to Sir Hubert Guest. 'No further

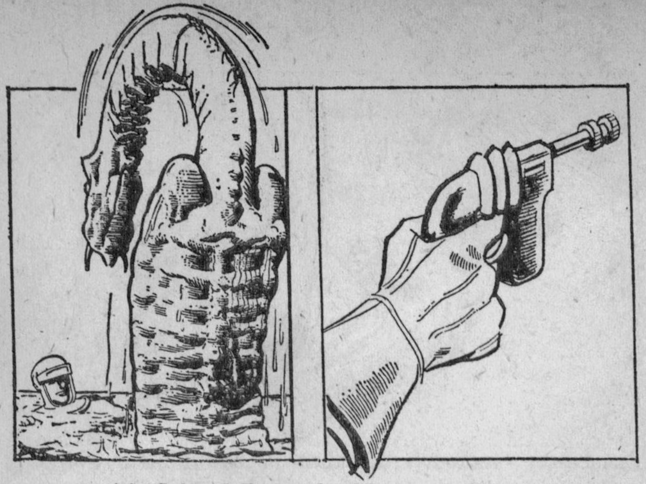

contact with Colonel Dare, sir. May we have permission to proceed, please?'

Sir Hubert gritted his teeth. 'Right, Pierre. I'll give you ten minutes and then follow.'

Pierre Lafayette licked his lips. 'I hope it's only a case of Dan's radio breaking down, Hank . . . '

Hank nodded slowly as the French-Canadian gunned the engines that sent them hurtling forward. 'But it was more than radio breakdown with *Orion*, *Argonaut* and *Kingfisher*, Pierre. Dan's theory *sounded* fine . . . but it could've been nuts.'

'Well, mon ami, we shall soon find out! Here we go!'

Sir Hubert Guest watched them go. 'That's two ships away, Miss Peabody. If we don't hear anything from them in *five* minutes, I'll return to *Ranger*, put you aboard, and then come back and make the third pass solo.'

'Put me on *Ranger*?' The girl's voice exploded angrily. 'Not likely! I'm staying on this mission whatever happens – and you can court martial me for it if you like!'

Sir Hubert shrugged wearily, tired of arguing with this firebrand . . .

Meanwhile, far below, Spaceman Digby clawed himself clear of the mud into which he'd made a messy crashdown, after narrowly missing the craggy rocks at the edge of the Venusian Sea. He wiped the ooze from his helmet visor and scowled round him. 'Uggh! Beastly stuff! It's just like treacle!'

Awkwardly, he scrambled up the rocks until he reached a

pinnacle from which he could scan the surrounding areas. His eyes found Dan Dare's parachute almost at once, drifting slowly ashore, but then they widened with horror as he saw the commotion in the water not fifty yards distant! The lashing body of some huge, reptilian creature, churning the surface to foam as it fought with something he knew only too well to be his colonel!

But Dan was in less trouble than his tubby batman thought! Massive the sea-monster might have been – but its brain, like that of so many gigantic creatures, was tiny. Easily, he dodged the thrashing attacks of the cumbersome beast – although he knew that once hit by any part of the enormous head, he'd be battered into unconsciousness!

Cool as ice, Dan Dare backed off and drew the paralysing pistol from his belt. 'If this is your welcome, you overgrown refugee from Loch Ness . . . ' He pulled the trigger, and a lancing ray of powerful force smashed into the monster's neck! There was an ear-shattering bellow of rage and fear before its muscles locked rigid and it slid slowly beneath the turbulence . . .

'Are you all right, sir?' Digby had come scrambling down the rocks again, and Dan waved a reassuring hand as he stumbled through the shoreline ooze to join him. 'I'm okay, Dig. And you?'

'Fair to middling, sir. But I've taken a look round, and I don't see any bus stops or snack bars around here!'

'Ah! You mean, "what do we do next", eh, Dig?' Dan clapped his batman on the shoulder. 'Well, we've somehow got to cross a large slice of this planet, because one of the other ships may get through, and we had a rendezvous planned in the permanent twilight zone.' Dan fished a small gadget from a zipped pocket in his outer suit and clipped it to his wrist. 'This is an infra-red guidance compass, set on the rendezvous point. All we have to do is follow it.'

Digby gulped. 'But – but it's pointing out to *sea*, Colonel Dan!'

'So it is, Digby! We're going to have to build ourselves a boat!'

Far beyond them, Number Three rocketship was approaching the force-field danger area. All at once, Hank Hogan snapped his fingers! 'Cut the engines, Pierre! At once!'

Pierre Lafayette knew his American colleague too well to waste time asking questions. He did as he was told. 'What's up, mon brave?'

'Turn back for Sir Hubert. There's an idea I've had – a notion concerning Dan. I want to check it out before we make our attempt to bust through.'

'Okay, Hank. Mind telling an old friend what it is?'

'It's to do with the radio. I think I know why Dan's one packed up . . . '

CHAPTER FOUR

# THE TREENS!

There were trees bordering the shore-line of the Venusian Sea, smooth, soft-timbered trunks that grew in profusion where the grim pile of crag-like rocks petered out. Together, Dan and Digby had felled more than half a dozen of them, using special settings on their pistols to send out lance-like cutting rays. With creepers, they had lashed the resulting logs together into a serviceable raft.

'How about oars, Colonel Dan?' said Digby mournfully. 'An' how long do you think we'll have to paddle?'

'Forget oars, Dig,' said Dan. He glanced at the leaves of the still-standing trees, gauging the direction of the wind. 'We'll be under sail. Nip back and collect my parachute, will you?'

When Digby returned, puffing under the weight of the silk, Dan had a crude mast rigged. He'd also removed his spacesuit. 'I've been checking the atmosphere. High carbon dioxide, but otherwise okay. So strip down to normal clothes, and just keep your helmet on.'

The strange craft blew straight off-shore, and by hauling on the strings of the parachute he'd harnessed to his mast, Dan kept the vessel on course, constantly glancing down at the infra-red compass. He was so intent on his task that it was quite some time before he realised that Digby had actually gone to sleep!

'Hoi! Wake up, you lump of Lancashire lard! Here we are on a new and unexplored planet, and all *you* can do is go to kip!'

Digby spluttered. 'Ee – I was only conserving me strength, sir!'

'Well, consider it conserved. There's land ahead!'

The raft ground up on to a shingly shore, backed by great towering walls of rock incised with vertical chasms that hinted at canyons, and pocked with caves.

There was no sign of life to greet the wary explorers, but as they made their way forward, a patter of rocks came tumbling down towards them.

'Oh – oh! We don't want to be flattened by a landslide, Dig! Come on – up this gully!'

They halted suddenly. In front of them, as if guarding the entrance to a cave, was a tall pillar of smooth stone. It bore no markings of any kind, but something – some instinct – told Dan that it was no natural formation!

'Something – some*body* made that, Digby. I think we'd better be ready for anything!'

Digby followed close after his colonel as Dan stepped boldly into the cave. 'F-funny . . .' The batman swallowed hard. 'F-funny how you get the feeling you're being *watched* . . .'

A lizard's beady eyes flashed suddenly from a ledge alongside and made him jump. Something like a bat flapped past him and out into the open behind them. And from a niche far above them in the cave's interior, the glittering stare of a being. A humanoid! Lank hair fell to the man's shoulders, masking a clean-shaven face whose lines were drawn taut with malevolent hostility! Beneath the strange bump on the forehead of the blue-skinned alien the eyes glittered evilly.

The watcher waited for no more than a minute. Abruptly, he turned and ran softly and silently down a rocky passageway which brought him out in sight of a huge building, set in the depths of a canyon. There were guards at the gate – guards in the company of some kind of officer, who stood with folded arms, watching the runner's approach.

Haughtily, the officer listened as the watcher gasped out his story. Then he snapped his fingers and barked an order, and instantly, doors slid back to reveal a weird machine that was all too obviously some kind of war vehicle! As their officer stepped inside, helmeted soldiers of the blue-skinned race clambered aboard, and the thing began to move . . .

It came suddenly, as Dan and Digby were still examining the cave. Dan had found inscriptions on the walls – hieroglyphics that had given him the certain knowledge of intelligent life on Venus. For his part, Digby had found and made friends with a small lizard. He'd just christened it John Willie when he looked up and froze. There, at the entrance to the cave, stood the soldiers, guns cradled ready in their hands!

Afterwards, Digby was surprised that he kept so calm. 'Don't look now, sir, but we've been followed. By a bunch of over-

grown bluebottles,' was all he had said, and added, 'To coin a phrase, the natives appear to be hostile!'

Digby already had his pistol drawn, but Dan laid a cautioning hand on his arm. 'Don't shoot, Dig. I'll try and talk to them . . . '

'Don't be daft, sir! The only talking you'll do to that bunch of heathens will be famous last words –and they won't appreciate 'em!'

Dan grimaced. 'Stop nattering, Dig. Just keep me covered.'

Fearlessly, the colonel stepped forward, his hands raised in the universal gesture of unarmed friendship . . . and without the slightest warning, a blast of concussive power shot from the gun of one of the guards and dropped him in his tracks!

With a roar of dismayed fury, Digby launched himself forward! Now his gun came up, and the stunning force of it swept around the startled aliens! Incredibly, they couldn't have expected retaliation of any sort, and they froze where they stood – mere statues under the power of the temporarily paralysing ray that Digby had used!

'Colonel Dan! Colonel Dan!' The tubby batman was on his knees beside his beloved chief. '*Speak* to me!' Then the lad from Wigan shouted in pure relief! Dan's eyes were flickering open!

'Help – help me, Dig! Just knocked flat – for a second! Their guns may be big and noisy, but – but they don't have that much power!'

As Digby helped Dan to his feet, his eyes swept round the

blue-skinned soldiers in their frozen stances. 'I didn't get 'em all, sir! At least two got clear . . . '

Carefully, they took a closer look at their enemies. 'They're so human, Dig . . . yet they don't wear dome helmets. How can they breathe in this carbon dioxide atmosphere . . . ?'

Digby approached the officer of the group. The one who wore a tall, almost cylindrical hat, reminiscent of the headgear of an ancient Egyptian pharaoh. 'I reckon this one's the guv'nor, sir. Proper bilious-lookin', isn't he! I'd hate to be one of his merry men when the paralysis wears off in a couple of hours!'

The batman added, 'And maybe *we'd* better make ourselves scarce before the rest of the lads of the village turn up!'

As they stepped out into the open, they saw the huge war vehicle parked there. Dan smiled. 'Seems they've left us their transport . . . '

'Aye, sir. If we can find out where it's wound up, we can use it . . . '

But then, even as Dan and Digby began to approach the vehicle, a noise behind and above them made them whirl! They had no chance to use their guns, for as they lifted them, a score of blue-skinned bodies dropped from the rocks to send them crashing to the dirt in a tangle of struggling arms and legs! Smothered and helpless, they felt their senses slip away under the sheer pressure of their opponents . . .

Dan and Digby came to slowly. Aware that their hands had

been tied behind them, they were also conscious of movement. As full realisation flooded back, they knew they were in the war-machine, speeding headlong over the rocky terrain on some kind of hover principle. Digby was just opening his mouth to say something when the whole contraption suddenly dived from the edge of a cliff and plummeted down towards the sea!

'Yieeeee!' The batman screwed his eyes shut and waited for the crash – but it never came! Next instant, the machine was scudding across the water, turning swiftly, hugging the coast. And then it slowed, and before them loomed the strange, towering immensity of some alien city, with an entrance ramp that curved up from the ocean surface!

'Well, this seems to be it, Dig.' Dan Dare looked unnaturally tense as the vehicle zoomed up the steep ramp. 'I wonder what's in store for us now . . . '

'Better ask for the manager, sir,' quavered Digby.

The vehicle slid to a halt within an immense entrance chamber. Dan and Digby were hustled out and then, powerless to resist, though they struggled manfully against the opposition, they felt blue hands snatching at the fastenings of their helmets!

'No! *No*, you fools! *We can't breathe carbon dioxide*!'

It would be a horrible, choking end. Starved of precious oxygen! A bloated, gasping death of maybe five minutes' horrifying duration . . . or would it? Amazingly, Dan realised that the atmosphere was not $CO_2$ at all! He shook his head to

clear the numbness of shock from his brain. 'Phew! Relax, Dig! It – it smells fine. It's air right enough. The odd tang in it must have fooled our tester . . . '

Then they saw that their captors had fallen to the floor, heads bowed as if in worship. And from the darkness at the back of the vaulted chamber, a tall, statuesque figure was approaching.

'Crikey, Colonel Dan! Now what? Who's *this*? He ain't one of the bluebottles! Look – his skin's green, and he's wrapped up in some sort of shiny suit like a bloomin' mummy!'

The figure halted. His angular, almost reptilian green face glared at them. And from all around the room came the concerted, devotional moan of the blue aliens. 'Treen! Treen!' The chant of worship rose to an ear-splitting crescendo! *TREEEEENNNN!*'

There was silence, then. A silence that, after what seemed to Dan an interminable pause, the newcomer spoke.

'Colonel Dare and Spaceman Digby, I presume!'

## CHAPTER FIVE

# FOR EXPERIMENTAL PURPOSES

'This way, gentlemen. Don't worry about your helmets. You will not need them any more.' The being stood impassively, seeming to betray little interest in Dan and Digby.

'How – how on earth do you speak English?' Dan was frankly incredulous. 'How do you know our names?'

'I am a Treen,' shrugged the being. 'We Treens have studied the earth for twenty-six thousand years, and every Treen child knows all its languages. Now – as I ordered – step this way.'

The Treen led them through to another chamber where a massive glass ball dominated the centre of the floor. A touch of a control button on a side-mounted console proved it to be a type of three-dimensional television receiver, and Dan and Digby gasped as a perfect image came up within it. It was the image of Number Three rocketship, manned by Hank Hogan and Pierre Lafayette, and their own radio signals to Sir Hubert Guest were coming over, loud and clear!

'We're heading in now, sir! The radio has been jettisoned, and so we should have no trouble from the force-field!'

'Good old Pierre,' grinned Dan, oblivious for an instant of his own predicament. 'He and Hank must've worked it out! Happy landings, lads!'

'It was unfortunate for you, Colonel Dare,' interrupted the

Treen, 'that you yourself landed among humans. That was your greatest hazard.'

'Did you say *humans* . . . ?'

The Treen nodded. 'Yes. They have, alas, never outgrown their digestions, emotions, or fighting instincts. We leave them alone, except when we wish to use them as slaves.'

'Do – do you mean those blue jobs came from Earth . . . ?' Dan couldn't keep the amazement out of his voice.

'Their ancestors were brought back for research from a space-ship survey many, many thousands of years ago. They speak only their own language, and tend to attack strangers.'

'You can say that again,' breathed Digby.

'We have watched your efforts to penetrate our ray barrier with some amusement,' continued the Treen, changing the subject abruptly. 'Now, why don't you pay attention to the screen and watch your foolhardy friends come to grief?'

'They're smarter than we were,' said Dan. 'They've ditched their radio.'

'Ah – but they happen to be heading for the flamelands of our equator, Colonel Dare. Our hemispheres are divided by a molten belt, and for centuries we have had little contact with the south. I am afraid the course your friends have chosen will take them into this area. They will not survive.'

'Do you believe him, Colonel Dan?' Digby sounded horrified.

'I believe him, Digby . . . ' Dan, bound though he was, jerked forward and thrust his body against the controls of the three-dimensional screen. It went dead. 'But I don't want to watch!'

'Pah! Emotional nonsense,' scoffed the Treen. 'But we waste time. I have orders to fetch you by electrosender to Mekonta, the capital of our hemisphere.'

Contemptuously, as though he was super-confident that these mere earthmen, disarmed as they were, could do him no harm, the Treen loosed their bonds, and conducted them to where a long, bullet-shaped vessel lay within the confines of a glass-like tube.

'The electrosender, gentlemen! The car is drawn along by a series of electromagnets. The tube is a vacuum, and we reach speeds up to fifteen thousand earth miles per hour . . . '

The friends stepped inside. Neither of them, full as they were of the deaths of Hank and Pierre, had the heart to make any comment about the incredible advancement of Treen technology.

Mekonta. Capital of the northern hemisphere of Venus. The home of the Treens. A vast city built on floating islands in an artificially calmed lake. Islands criss-crossed by canals filled with the vari-coloured water of the planet. Neither Dan nor Digby had ever dreamed of such a place. Such a fantastic layout of futuristic buildings. Such monumental structures, their shapes interlaced with pylon-suspended travel-tubes such as the one that brought them there. The lower skies were dotted with

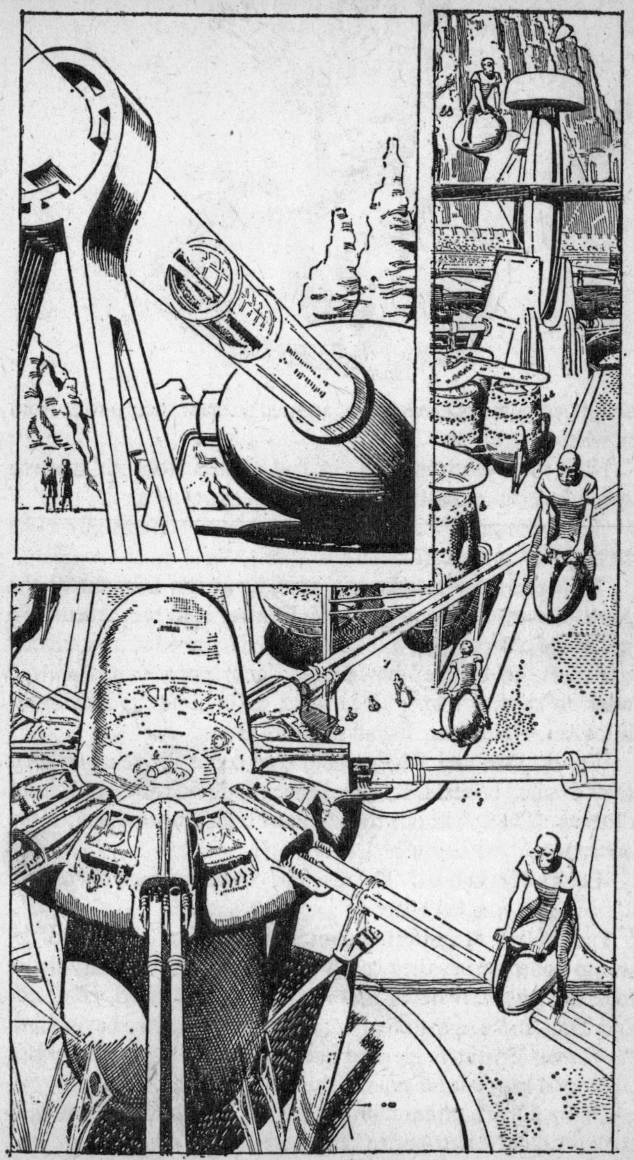

small personal hoverbikes that seemed to draw their power from nowhere.

Now their electrosender car had slowed from its amazing speed and came coasting in towards a central area . . .

'Where to now?' Dan looked about him wonderingly as he stepped from the car.

'My orders are to take you straight to the Director of the Earth Observatory and Research Centre,' said the Treen. 'We use flying chairs – you will have noticed them – for internal city transport. Of course,' he sneered, 'your puny brains are too weak to control them. They work on concentrated thought-impulses. No matter. I shall guide all three.'

Warily, Dan and Digby clambered on to the seats of what they'd called hoverbikes. The Treen mounted another, in front of them. Then, without the slightest effort on the part of the earthmen, the weird vehicles took off!

'Look! No hands!' The curious situation was having an almost light-headed effect on Digby!

Past towers of glittering glass and concrete, past buildings whose composition they could only guess at, the flying chairs took the prisoners down into the city. At last, all three dived, and Dan and Digby swept into a sort of landing bay behind the Treen. Instinctively, the batman ducked his head, fearful that he'd knock it off against the roof!

Digby fell off, rather than got off, his hoverbike. Instantly, it took off again! 'Hey-oop! Come back, Humphrey!'

'They return automatically,' snapped the Treen. 'Now come, both of you. We must not keep the Director waiting!'

'Look.' Dan spoke evenly. 'Do you mind if I ask you just why this Director chappie wants to see us?'

The Treen's face betrayed not one flicker of emotion. 'For interrogation, gentlemen. For interrogation and – experiment.'

'Experiment!' Digby echoed the Treen's words. 'I can't say I like the sound of that, Colonel Dan!'

'Neither do I, Digby. Not in the least! But one thing's clear. We're stuck in the middle of Mekonta – and there's precious little we can do about our situation at the moment. We just have to play everything by ear.' As an afterthought, he said, 'I know it's asking a lot, Dig – but whatever happens, keep cool. While there's life, and all that . . . '

A strange and chilling sight greeted the eyes of the two friends as they were at length forced into the presence of the Director of Research. This was a high, vaulted room in which machines of sinister, even evil purpose were ranged around a central dais. And on that dais stood a man – the virtual replica of their captor. All these Treens seemed to look exactly alike! Dan and Digby both shivered as they felt themselves under the close scrutiny of the other watchers who studied their approach with such spine-tingling detachment. 'It's – it's just as though we were a couple of specimens on a microscope slide, sir,' whispered Digby. 'Just specimens to be analysed and – oh my gosh – maybe *dissected*!'

'Let me look at them.' The Director stepped from the dais and walked round the captives. Digby thought that the head-gear he wore – presumably to distinguish himself as a leader – was ridiculous. His uncontrolled smirk showed it. 'You see something to amuse you, earthman?'

'Aye, mate. You could make a rare bedside lamp out o' that titfer! Got a spare I can take home to me Auntie Anastasia?'

Inwardly, Dan blessed Digby for his irrepressible humour. No danger that the tubby batman would crack up under the strain! As for the Director, he was typically unmoved.

'You will laugh on the other side of your faces in due course. But that will be later. At present, I am not quite ready for you.' He turned to their captor. 'Take them away and feed them. I will let you know when all the preparations have been completed.'

'Yes, Director!' The Treen bowed, and Dan and Digby were led out of the chamber again.

'Food, eh?' said Digby. 'Oh well, the condemned men always eat a hearty breakfast, Colonel Dan!'

Neither Dan nor Digby believed particularly in miracles. Which was a pity, for in fact, one had happened. Perhaps it was lucky that Dan had shut off the three dimensional television screen, or their Treen captor might have seen what actually happened when rocketship Three had dived into the terrifying inferno of the Venus flame-belt!

Rock-steady at the controls, Pierre Lafayette had refused to panic. Though the temperature in the cabin had risen to an almost intolerable level, he'd managed to pull the machine up and away from the holocaust. Dizzily, the craft had plunged onwards and into the clear skies of the southern Hemisphere of Venus. Then – and only then – with a long stretch of lake below him, had Pierre given way. He slumped forward against the sprawled, already senseless figure of his companion, and the rocketship had gone into a shallow dive . . .

As for rocketship One – Professor Peabody at the controls and the wildly agitated Sir Hubert Guest beside her – they'd come in, hard on Pierre's heels. But they'd seen what has happening to him just in time!

Expertly, the girl had wrestled the controls to bring the ship away from the flame-belt. The G-forces nearly made her black out, and she could hear her superior's feeble voice demanding that she let him take over! But she refused! Although her vessel was beyond her immediate influence, it was down through the atmosphere, and plummeting towards an angry, red-looking area on one side of the central equator. On the *northern* side . . . Hostile enough, environmentally – and though they didn't know it, within that part of Venus controlled by the Treens. But still they'd land in one piece. Still – they'd be alive.

Such were the miracles, about which Dan and Digby knew nothing. And as Dan had said – even knowing that he was going to be used as some kind of experimental guinea-pig – while there's life, there's hope!

CHAPTER SIX

## A FIGHTING CHANCE!

On the way to what he called 'the food chamber', the Treen guiding Dan and Digby paused at a large pair of sliding doors. 'You have museums on earth, humans. Perhaps you would like a glimpse at part of ours? It is a fractional part of our collection, of course, but this particular section will give you an idea of . . .' he paused, and Dan had the impression that if a Treen's face were capable of registering emotion, this one would show smugness '. . . Treen thoroughness!'

The Treen pressed a switch, and the two friends gasped as their eyes took in the extraordinary scene before them

'By gum,' breathed Digby. 'Old aircraft! Perfect replicas of military uniforms, right down through the ages! It's uncanny, Colonel Dan!'

'Some of the items,' said the Treen, 'we reconstructed ourselves from careful observation. Others, we actually captured. You will be aware that, from time to time on your planet, there have been reports of unidentified flying objects. You call them saucers, I believe. Well, such things were of course Treen craft.'

'Fascinating!' Dan was impressed, despite himself. He nudged his batman and pointed to a pair of dummies, clad in

uniforms of the Interplanetary Space Fleet. 'Pretty well our size, Dig! I think we might do a spot of borrowing if the opportunity presents itself!'

'Have you got a plan then, sir?'

Dan inclined his head slightly, and Digby smiled at the twinkle in the colonel's eye.

'Come, then,' said the Treen. 'The food chamber.'

The place was in an ante-room just beyond the museum entrance. There were devices there like tall goldfish bowls, linked to consoles which were pumping a clear liquid into two of them.

'You will immerse yourselves in those food baths,' ordered their escort. 'thirty seconds will be enough to give you all the nourishment you need.'

'You mean we absorb grub, through our skins? I'd much rather have some black puddin' and chips,' glowered Digby. But the Treen didn't seem to hear him as he strode away and left them to it.

'Come on, Dig. I dare say it'll satisfy our hunger, like he said. These characters seem to have everything pretty well taped.' Dan stripped off and clambered into one of the tanks.

'What do you make of these green horrors, Colonel Dan?' Digby glanced across at his chief from the next tank.

'Well, they're quite inhuman, Dig. And clearly, they've got unpleasant plans for us. But we must remember why we're here on Venus. and string along with them for the time being.

I'm going to do my darndest to find out whether there's any hope that they'll come to a peaceful arrangement to send food to the earth.'

'Is that why you've got your eye on those uniforms, sir?'

'Exactly, Digby! Wearing them, we'll feel much more like a pair of envoys from the United World Government. There's nothing like a uniform to give a chap a sense of authority!'

Their food baths over, the friends discarded their space undersuits and rigged themselves out in style. The uniforms did fit pretty well – and Digby was especially well pleased! 'Heh, heh, Colonel – I've got a reet step up the ladder! From Spaceman class one to full captain in one easy go!'

'Ha! No need to get ideas, Dig. Although if we ever *do* come out of this in one piece, you'll have promotion sure enough! Now put a jaunt in your step and a tilt in your hat! It's time we stopped letting these Treens push us round so much!'

If the Treen Director of Research felt any surprise at his captives' new outfits, he had no difficulty in concealing it. Digby felt his vanity pricked when the man, having had them summoned back to his presence, hardly gave him a second glance!

'I am ready to begin my experiments! First I will spectro-analyse them. Fasten the fat one to the slide . . . '

Then Dan stepped forward, his voice ringing clearly and commandingly in the vast, vaulted chamber! 'Stop!'

Some of the Treen guards moved forward menacingly, but the Director waved them back. 'Stop?'

'We're here as official envoys of the United World Government,' said Dan sternly. 'I demand that you take us immediately

to the Chief Officer of your state. Your president or Prime Minister or whoever corresponds to that!'

'You mean the Mekon? The Mekon of Mekonta? The supreme scientist – the Illustrious One of Venus?'

'That's right,' chipped in Digby. 'We want to see the gaffer!'

There was no anger in the Director's face, for Treens did not show such things. But his words were scathing!

'Obscure insects from backward planets such as yours would not even be allowed to enter the same building as that magnificent brain! Your only interest to the Mekon is as biological specimens for my earth research!' He snapped his fingers. 'Fasten them to the slides!'

Then came a sudden interruption. A Treen ran into the chamber, halting respectfully in front of the director. 'Master! The third rocketship has crashed into the molten fringe of the flamelands – on the northern edge!'

'We have two specimens,' shrugged the Director. 'We do not need more.'

'But one of these is a woman, master . . . '

'Indeed.' The Director sounded interested. He seemed to ponder for long moments before he came to a decision. 'Release the specimens,' he ordered. 'We will study their reactions and impulses while they watch the peril of their friends!'

Dan and Digby had already been strapped into what the Director had called 'slides' – actually chair-like contrivances which held them fast imprisoned, their heads covered with some

kind of helmet containing sophisticated electronic probes. Now they were wheeled forward to face the familiar globe of a three-dimensional television screen, and on it they could clearly see Number One rocketship.

'Cut in the audio monitors,' snapped the Director. 'Let us hear what is going on inside the vessel!'

Attendants did his bidding, and the voice of Sir Hubert Guest flooded the room. 'Are you all right, Miss Peabody?'

'I – I think so, sir! One thing – the ship seems to have survived impact!'

Dan writhed in his seat, but found he could hardly move. In front of him, the image of the crashed spacecraft, nose-down in a hot and smoking ooze . . .

Inside the ship, Sir Hubert reached up for the escape hatch. 'I'm going ashore to reconnoitre.'

'I'm coming too,' said the girl.

Sir Hubert's face flushed beneath the dome of his space helmet. 'On the contrary, Miss Peabody! Under no circumstances will you leave this ship until I return! This time, consider it a direct order!'

Reluctantly, the girl stayed put as Sir Hubert thrust himself on to the shell of the ship. It took him seconds to set the controls of his atmospheric analysis device.

'Hmm. Gaseous silicon. Darned high temperature, too. Highly unhealthy!'

He moved carefully to the uptilted rear of the craft. 'Jets clogged. We'd probably explode if we started the engines to clear them. And hang it, we're slowly *sinking*!' He peered down at the thick ooze below. Saw the line of it creeping ever upwards along the vessels' smooth flanks.

And in that instant, Sir Hubert Guest slipped! One moment he was on the metal skin – the next, up to his ankles in the hot, shifting material below!

He scarcely had time to yell before he felt strong arms seize him under the armpits! And then Professor Jocelyn Peabody was heaving him back to safety!

'It's a good thing I disobeyed your – ah – direct order, Sir Hubert!' She was panting, but Sir Hubert couldn't help feeling amazement at the strength in this person he'd dismissed as a mere woman!

'You'd be up to your neck in that stuff by now,' continued the girl.

'Hrmmmf. I know it. Thank you, Miss Peabody. However, I don't see that it makes that much difference . . . ' He smiled hastily, realising that he was perhaps being a little too ungracious. 'Fact is, we're sinking steadily, and in no more than a few hours we'll have to choose between roasting, exploding or suffocating!' Sir Hubert was about to add a plea to his companion not to panic. The last thing he wanted in this predica-

ment was a hysterical female on his hands, he told himself. But the thought died in his mind as he glanced at her and saw the calm on her face.

'Sir Hubert – ' Jocelyn Peabody's voice had a sudden edge to it. 'Look over there. There's a – a sort of *glass mountain* thing. And it's moving towards us!'

'Glass mountain? Good grief, you're right! Whatever can it be? Some kind of silicon compound, judging by the atmosphere . . . but it appears to be swallowing the rocks around it! As if it were *alive* . . . !'

'Is it possible?' Professor Peabody repressed a shudder of horror. And the terrifying mass rolled nearer!

As they watched the ghastly spectacle on the television screen in Mekonta, Dan Dare found it impossible to keep silent any longer! 'We *have* to rescue them!'

'Why, Colonel Dare?' The Director was still infuriatingly

bland. 'Their deaths will be more instructive than their lives.'

But it seemed that one of his assistants – a senior one, or he would never have dared to question the Director's authority – disagreed.

'Why not *let* them try to rescue their comrades, master? With four of them, we could carry out much greater research. And – as the messenger pointed out – one *is* a woman. Her reactions might be different, and interesting.'

'Hm. That is so,' mused the Director. 'But how would they do it?' He thought long and deeply, while Dan strove in vain to conceal his impatience.

At last the Treen spoke, and Dan could scarcely repress a gasp of relief! 'Colonel Dare, I have decided to let you bring in your comrades from their present, rather warm situation . . . '

The Director continued. 'Unfortunately, our main methods of communication do not extend to the flame-belt. You will be taken by telesender to the main part of our museum – the Hall of Machines. You can take your pick of the transport there.'

Released from their chairs, Dan and Digby – the latter replacing his captain's peaked cap with cool dignity – were shown to a pair of vertical glass tubes, the end pair in a whole row of such things that stood to one side of the chamber. Treens opened the doors of these units, and the friends were placed inside.

'You need have no fear of the telesenders, gentlemen,' said the Director. 'See – I shall take my place in a third, and we will

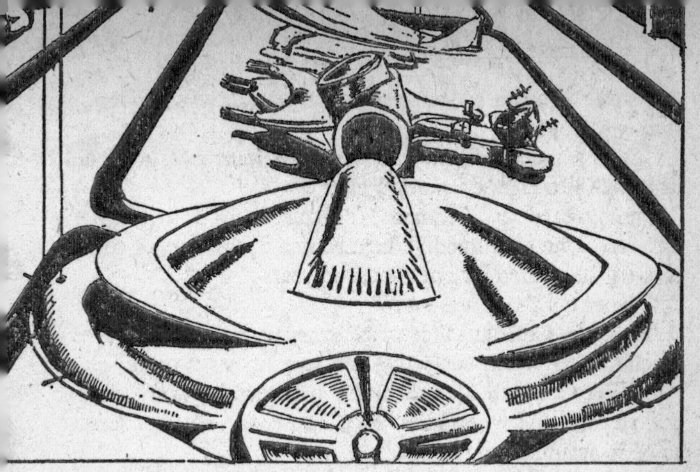

be de-materialised. Our entire metabolisms will be transported to another part of this area in the blink of an eye. It is a most convenient form of travel, I assure you.'

'I'm hanged if *I* like the ideas of it,' Digby grumbled. 'Are you sure we'll turn up at our destination with all our parts assembled properly? I don't want to have to go round with me feet on top of me head for the rest of me life!'

The doors were closed. There was the brief sight of a Treen technician pressing a button on a control console, and then – just as the Director had said – in the blink of an eye they were elsewhere! There was just one thing . . .

Furious at being re-materialised upside down, Digby spluttered and groused as the Director helped him out. 'These technical hitches *do* happen occasionally,' the Treen said evenly.

'But why always to me?' blazed the tubby batman.

Dan wasn't listening. He was gazing about him in fascination at the vast array of transport in the museum. Transport of all conceivable types. Old-fashioned aircraft, helicopters, saucers, rockets and ferry-ships. An incredible collection that absolutely beggared description!

'We'll need to use something pretty fast to get us there in time,' said Dan. It was difficult to focus his eye on any one machine, so bewildering was the variety.

'Don't worry, Colonel Dare. We have every machine from four planets. Perhaps this one might serve your purpose . . . ' The Director strode across and pointed up at a bulbous, fish-like pod slung beneath a completely circular link of cylinders. A kind of jetcopter?

'Judging by the flame-belt, what we want is a good old-fashioned fire-engine,' snorted Digby.

Dan ignored his batman. He glanced enquiringly at the Director, who continued. 'The machine is obsolete, of course. Has not been used for one thousand years . . . '

'Then how the blazes . . . ?'

'Patience, Colonel! This place is hermetically sealed. Every machine here works perfectly. You have my word on it.'

A Treen's word? Dan shook his head gently, wondering at this strange and emotionless race whose only interest seemed to be in scientific knowledge.

'Right, then,' he said. 'Let's have it made ready. And quickly.'

That was no problem. Within a moment, a gang of Treens were fitting capsules to the body of the machine. 'Fluorine sprays,' explained the Director. 'To neutralise the silicon mass. You may as well enter, gentlemen. The jetcopter will be ready to be moved out in precisely one minute.'

Dan and Digby scaled a ladder that led into the ship's interior, to stop short suddenly.

'Hullo,' said Digby. 'There's already someone here!'

At the controls, the tall figure of a Treen turned towards them impassively. 'I am to pilot you,' he said. 'You will also be watched by televiewer.'

The Treen turned back to his unit as the entry-port closed, and slowly, the jetcopter began to taxi towards the airlock exitway at one end of the vast museum building. The noise of its progress dinned in the confines of the place, and Dan put his lips close to Digby's ear to make himself heard. What he said was for his batman alone!

'This could be it, Dig! The Treens are so confident of their own superiority, I reckon they've blundered! If we can rescue Sir Hubert and the Professor, then overcome this pilot, we can take over this transport! Watch the controls so's we know how to fly the thing when the time comes!'

'Bang on, sir!' Digby couldn't keep the excitement out of his voice as he whispered back. 'Looks like we've wangled ourselves a fighting chance!'

CHAPTER SEVEN

## BID FOR FREEDOM!

The jetcopter drove upwards and away from Mekonta, the city dwindling behind until it was lost over the horizon. Somewhere ahead lay the perils of the flamelands, which the pilot said they'd reach in slightly less than an hour.

'Why not have a go at him now, Colonel Dan?' Digby was whispering again in his chief's ear. 'Hold your horses, Dig! We'll play things my way. As a matter of fact, I'm going to have a go at making friends with old green-face up there!'

'With him? A Treen? You must be joking, sir! Ee – I don't think there'll be anything palsy-walsy about him!'

Dan was nonetheless determined to try. Win or lose, it mattered little to his plans. But as Dig predicted, the Treen wasn't very forthcoming!

'Why do you extend your hand to me, Colonel Dare? I, Sondar, see nothing logical in it.'

Sondar turned back to his controls. 'As I understand it, the giving of hands is an ancient earth gesture to show one does not carry arms. It is also used before boxing-matches, and by businessmen about to cheat one another!'

Dan shrugged. 'Quite a humorous observation,' he said. 'Not

that you meant it that way, I fancy. It's a great pity, in my view, that you Treens, with all your brilliance, have neglected such things as friendship, and feelings . . . '

Sondar crushed him. 'Your view does not interest me, Colonel Dare. Now kindly make ready. We shall shortly be approaching the silicon mass. This ancient machine seems to fly faster than at first I imagined.'

Dan returned to Digby, who was craning to peer out of one of the jetcopter's side-screens. 'Look down there, sir! I can see the rocketship! Bang in the middle of that thing that looks like an outsize humbug!'

'That's not a bad description, Dig! But the silicon mass seems to be eating the ship! I don't know whether it's possible that Sir Hubert and the Professor are still alive! They aren't on top of the hull any more!'

Now Sondar's voice cut in. 'Hang on. I am going to bank over the target zone. I shall switch on the fluorine sprays – now!'

Inside the roasting hull of Number One rocketship, the two humans were very much alive. But with no idea of the presence of the jetcopter, they had just about given up hope of survival!

'The hull's beginning to fracture, Sir Hubert!' Professor Peabody's face was pouring sweat under her helmet as the temperature-equalisers of her suit started to give up the unequal struggle with the heat of their surroundings.

'Then there's nothing else for it. We'll have to fire the retro engines and take the risk of explosion. One thing's certain – if we do go up, we won't know very much about it!'

The girl gulped. 'I'm game if you are, Sir!'

'Good man! I mean – er – well, you *know* what I mean, Miss Peabody. Here goes . . . '

Sir Hubert's hand poised for an instant, then came down towards the firing lever! He closed his eyes, involuntarily. But then, startlingly . . .

'Stop! Wait!'

In the nick of time, Sir Hubert Guest froze his hand. His head jerked round to where the girl was standing, her face close to one of the rocketship's observation ports.

'The silicon mass! Something's happening to it! It's receding! There's something being *sprayed* on it!'

'Are you – are *you* sure?'

'Come and see for yourself, sir! It's being *destroyed*!'

Sir Hubert clambered to the escape hatch. Since being gripped in the silicon mass, the rocketship had been hauled bodily from the morass, and now lay inert on the surface. 'I don't know what's going on out there, Miss Peabody – but I'm going topside for a look! This time, you'd better join me!'

As they struggled out, the girl pointed upwards. 'It – it's some weird kind of flying machine!'

'They seem to be lowering some sort of ladder! By jove, we're being rescued!' Sir Hubert's voice had risen to a shout.

The ladder – steel-clad nylon – snaked down towards them and clanged on the roasted hull. Sir Hubert grabbed it and thrust the rungs into Professor Peabody's hands. 'Up you go! The sooner we're out of here the better!'

Jocelyn Peabody had climbed no more than a couple of rungs before she stopped – so abruptly that Sir Hubert, hot on her heels, struck his head against her feet! Could it be? Had that voice from above *really* spoken her name?

'Dan! *Dan*, by all that's wonderful!' She almost lost her grip. Nearly fell. But then Dan Dare's hands were there to help her, and she was being hauled into the jetcopter.

'I don't believe it! I *can't* believe it! Oh, Dan! *Dan*!'

Gently, Digby disentangled the girl's arms from his colonel's blushing neck. 'Me too, miss! Don't forget old Digby!'

'Oh no, Digby! Digby! It's so good to see you both! I'd given up hope of *everything*!'

'So had I,' said Sir Hubert, typically masking his own feelings of relief with a show of his usual testiness. 'Would somebody care to help me aboard? If, that is, it's not too much trouble.'

'Sir Hubert!' Dan wrung the elderly man's gauntleted hand warmly. 'You must have gone through Hades! We saw everything. Telemonitored. We could even *hear* you!'

'Well here's something you didn't hear, my boy,' said Sir Hubert, and his face broke into a broad beam. He turned to Jocelyn Peabody, clapping her on the shoulders. 'My dear girl.

Forgive me for being a stupid old nitwit. If ever I thought women were frail and feeble, my mind's changed now! You came through our ordeal magnificently. Superbly! I might even have cracked up myself if it hadn't been for your steady nerve!'

Jocelyn Peabody gaped. Flushed. Then she found her tongue. 'I – I really don't know what to say, Sir Hubert!'

'Take your helmets off,' suggested Dan. 'Then you can make your reply nice and clearly. We don't need our suits here,' he added.

'Apparently not,' said Sir Hubert, shedding his helmet and seeming to see, for the first time, the Space Fleet uniforms Dan and Digby were wearing. 'Where did you get those? And, by the way, who is *that*?'

Sir Hubert pointed at Sondar, who had apparently taken little notice of the proceedings. He had known he could leave it to the remote telescanners in Mekonta to record the behaviour of these mere humans.

'He's one of our hosts,' said Dan. 'They call themselves Treens.'

'So what are they?'

'Boffins run wild, sir. And quite inhuman. They have no emotions at all. More to the point, they're not on our side.'

Sir Hubert frowned. 'What d'you mean? *Enemies*?'

'For want of a better term, yes.' Dan spread his hands. 'We're their prisoners for the moment. At least, the Treens think so. They require us for research!'

Disinterestedly, Sondar was moving the controls that would turn the jetcopter around. Dan spoke softly to his rescued friends.

'Now there are four of us, sir, I think we might have a go at our chum there. To tell you the truth, I've been dying to have a poke at one of those nasty green faces!'

Now Sondar turned. It seemed that he was capable of overhearing more than the humans had given him credit for! 'Pray do nothing foolish, earthmen. Your intentions are quite clear to us and believe me, you are powerless.'

'Confound it! Bang goes the element of surprise,' cursed Dan. 'But I'm still . . .'

A yell from Digby cut him short. 'Hey up, sir! That silicon mass has got itself together again! It's grabbed the perishin' ladder!'

The jetcopter lurched! It was true! Below them, the glass-like substance had boiled up anew on the ooze, and now it had them fast! 'Wind in, Sondar! Wrench it free!' Dan braced himself against the tilting wall!

Too late! And hauled over as they were, there was no hope of using the fluorine spray! Inexorably, they were drawn down against the power of their straining jets!

Dan's brain remained crystal clear. In one instant, he had full appreciation of their situation! 'Dive, Sondar! Dive! Slacken off the ladder so we can unship the drum and toss it out!'

There was no response! Dan swivelled towards the Treen, his jaw dropping open as, for the first time, he saw emotion on the smooth, reptilian face! And it was the emotion of fear! Of *panic*! Astoundingly, Sondar was beyond his own control, and remained rigid as the jetcopter strove to climb against the impossible tug of the monstrous silicon beneath them!

'Sorry, friend – but there's no time to waste!' Dan hurled himself bodily at the taut figure, his right fist swinging round in a curving arc that exploded against Sondar's jaw! The Treen cartwheeled from his seat, crashing back against the starboard bulkhead to lie still! Dan threw himself down in the pilot's place and thrust downwards on the climb lever! Instantly, the tension that threatened to haul the machine to pieces stopped, and Digby and Sir Hubert knocked away the clamps that held the ladder drum against the superstructure! It tumbled away, to be swallowed in the muck below, and as the door slammed

shut, Dan gunned the unfamiliar vehicle lurchingly away from their peril!

'By gum, that was close!' Digby mopped his streaming brow and sat heavily down on the floor. 'You did a good job on cabbage-chops, Colonel Dan!'

'He's coming round, Dig! Quick – take over the controls!' Dan slid from the seat again, for Sondar was lumbering dizzily to his feet, his hand grabbing for one of the freed ladder-clamps! The green face twisted in fury as he swung the metal on high and rushed to close with the Colonel!

Dan neatly sidestepped the clumsy rush and almost casually reached out to seize the wrist. Sondar performed a perfect somersault, his flying heels slamming off the jetcopter's roof. His body hit the deck with breath-robbing force as Professor Peabody and Sir Hubert skittered out of the way. Then he was up – and coming for Dan yet again!

'You don't learn very fast, Sondar,' gritted Dan. 'And I thought you Treens were quick on the uptake!' A fist like a rock shot out and stopped the pilot in mid-rush. The impact of bone on bone was like a thunderclap in the confines of the cabin! The Treen buckled at the knees and fell. And this time, he lay still.

Dan rubbed his stinging knuckles. 'So far so good. Change course, Dig. We're probably flying on a radar beam that'll take us back to Mekonta. And Mekonta *isn't* where we want to go!'

'Aye, sir! Wherever we end up can't be any worse than that!'

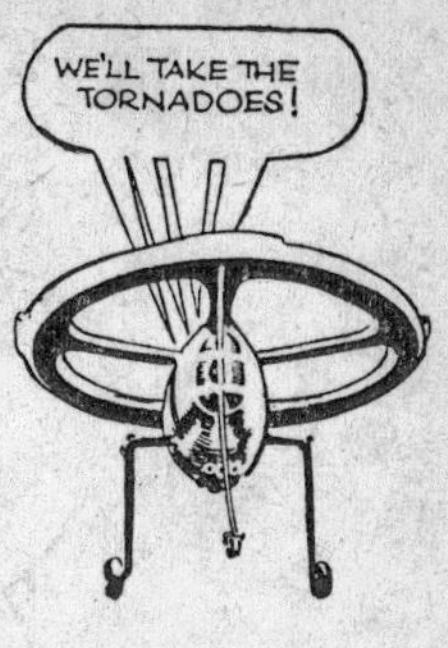


CHAPTER EIGHT

## PURSUIT – AND DISASTER!

The atmosphere in the vaulted chamber of Mekonta's Director of Research was deceptively quiet. The inbred calm of the Treens made the Director's reaction to the report he received absurdly matter-of-fact.

'So Sondar has broken off telecommunications, and the jetcopter is out of his control. Can it be that the earthmen have been unwise enough to pit their strength against us?'

'They are heading south, master. The fools must imagine that their miserable craft is able to cross the equatorial barrier.'

'They could be allowed to destroy themselves, I suppose. However, we need them alive. You will organise the raising of the tornado barrier!'

'At once, master!'

The astonishing technology of the Treens had long allowed them to exercise a fair amount of control over the elements. Now, invisible forces beamed from Mekonta set up a series of whirlwinds, each of incredible power, to be steered in pursuit of the fugitives! It was Digby who first saw them – cloud-high twisters of sucked-up rock and rubble, sweeping across the open plain to the north of the flamelands!

'By jove, they're moving fast!' Sir Hubert Guest watched as

the tornados spun away on both sides. All at once, the little craft felt very frail indeed!

'They can't be natural,' said Dan. 'It's Treen work, or I'm a Dutchman! The way they're being manoeuvred, it looks as though they're meant to cut us off – drive us back the way we came!'

'We could try a dash through . . . ' This was Digby. Then Professor Peabody said: 'Why not ask our green-faced friend? He's woken up.'

Sondar stared gloomily. 'Obviously we are required back at headquarters. For experiment of course.'

'You said "we"!' Dan was alert. 'You mean you as well?'

Sondar nodded. 'I displayed an emotion. Fear. When the ship was in danger. That was unscientific. They will want to analyse me and trace the fault.'

'Doesn't that beat all!' Digby laughed, shaking his head. 'Now he's in the same boat as we are! I reckon we don't want to have owt to do with those experiments at all, Colonel Dan. Let's take the tornados!'

'Hold tight, then! Let her rip, Digby!'

Nothing could compare with the battering inflicted on the tiny craft and its occupants as it shot bald-headed for the closest of the menacing tornados! The power of the jets was puny compared with the fearsome strength of the Treen-made wind that tore them upwards, flung them headlong, turned them over and over in the maelstrom of dust and debris until their senses

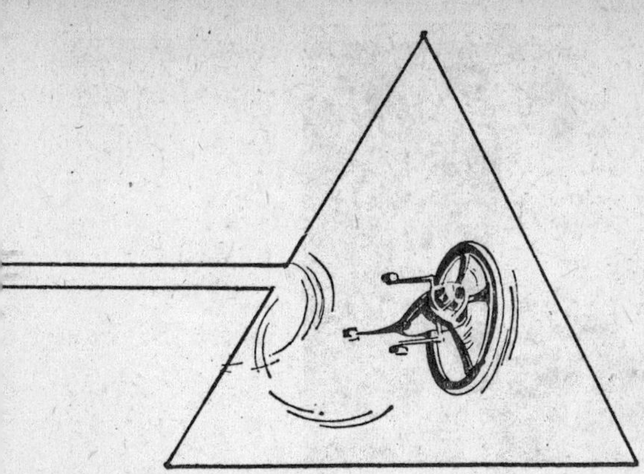

were shaken to nothing! Even with his own weight added to Digby's at the controls, Dan was helpless! Like a twisting toy, the jetcopter was spat from the summit of its whirling captor and sent, turning over and over, down towards the spinning ground – only to be plucked up anew!

'Enough! They are certain to crash! Turn off the tornados!' The Research Director glanced briefly away from the three-dimensional television. 'Electrosend guards to the estimated point of impact!'

His impassive gaze returned to the globe, watching the spinning columns of wind vanish as if they had never been there at all, watching as the broken, stricken jetcopter, its engines killed, fell headlong towards a tangle of thick jungle, well within the lands controlled by the Treens!

'They are hardy enough, these earthmen,' he mused. 'I imagine they will recover quickly enough from their shaking, severe though it may have been. *Prime* subjects for examination! Excellent!' He rubbed his bony hands together with satisfaction!

The wits of the fugitives returned slowly. Dazed and dizzy, they picked themselves up and stumbled on the impossibly tilted deck of their machine.

'We seem to have landed among trees.' Dan was the first to speak, brushing the mist from his eyes as he peered groggily out of the sight screens. 'The branches are like rubber. They've bent. Absorbed the shock of our impact without breaking. Luckily for us.'

'Not luck, Colonel Dare.' Sondar stood by his side. 'Design. The Director will deliberately have dropped us here in order that we might survive. There is an electrosender terminal near to this region,' he added.

'Thanks for telling us,' said Dan. 'That means the sooner we get down and away from the wreck, the better. Come on!'

'What about Sondar, Colonel Dan!?' Digby asked his chief.

'We'll take him with us – if he wants to come.' Dan raised his eyebrows at Sondar, who hesitantly nodded his head in agreement.

'Don't force yourself, chum,' said Digby.

Sondar shrugged – again a demonstration of some kind of emotion within him. 'Clearly, I am a failure as a Treen. Why should I not throw in my lot with you? I mean no treachery, I promise you.'

'You'd better not,' rapped Dan. 'Now come on. Out.'

It didn't take them long to scramble down the pliant branches of the tree that had broken their fall. There were supple creepers, too, and despite their situation, Dan had to smile as Digby – irrepressible as ever – did a restrained sort of Tarzan act to reach the jungle floor.

'How are we fixed for weapons?' Dan dusted himself down as he faced the others. 'Sir Hubert?'

'Miss Peabody and I both have our ray-pistols, Dan.'

'And I've got my infra-red compass.' The girl fished it out. 'Still set for the original rendezvous. We could strike out in that direction, just in case Hank and Pierre . . . '

Dan held up his hand. 'Not much hope of their survival, I'm afraid. We – we saw where they were headed.'

'If you will permit me,' said Sondar, 'I think we should head away from where I know the electrosender to be.'

'Jove, yes! I'd forgotten. Thank you once more, Sondar. You'd better lead . . . but believe me, any tricks and it'll be the worse for you!'

'Do you think we should trust him, Dan?' Sir Hubert frowned deeply.

'Tell me the alternative, Sir!'

Their eyes were momentarily off the Treen. That was why his sudden shout of terror snapped them round like marionettes! Sondar was backing away from a terrifying, snake-like monster of enormous size that had slid silently through the trees to rear over him! Its eyes stood out horribly, on stalks, an its mouth gaped to expose a jawful of spiny, razor-edged teeth!

Hypnotised and terrified, Sondar gazed up as the massive head began to strike! No sound escaped his lips save the dying whisper of his scream!

'Sir Hubert! Your pistol! *Quick!*'

Dan's yell spurred the older man to action. The gun came up to the aim, and a shattering bolt of energy burst from the barrel to slam the monster clean between those ghastly, protruding eyes!

The huge creature crashed backwards and lay still. Digby let out a whooping gasp of relief and ran to help Sondar to his feet. 'By gum, lad, but you are a proper wash-out as a Treen. You were proper panic-stricken, then. Just like me back home when City were about to score in the final minute!'

Sondar shook his head miserably. Now that they were in repose, his features looked somehow less sinister than those of his compatriots.

'Why? Why did you save me? You did not kill me in the jetcopter when you had the chance. Now you go so far as to rescue me from a terrible fate. Please – I do not understand such actions!'

Dan looked soberly at him and said nothing. Then, impulsively – and there was a definite hint of shame in his eyes – Sondar thrust out his awkward hand!

Dan took it, and smiled. 'Am I to understand that you may be recognising the idea of *friendship*, Sondar?'

The Treen looked away. 'It may be so. Never in thousands of years of our history has a Treen ever been allowed to change. It is – strange. I find it difficult to analyse my thoughts . . . '

'Lead on, Sondar,' said Dan kindly. 'And forget my threats. I don't think we have anything to fear from you. Not now.'

An hour and a half had passed. Panting with exertion, the five had trekked through the sweltering jungle, their eyes ever watchful for the savage wildlife lurking around them. But there had been no further trouble – at least, not from any living thing. Now, however, they found their way barred by a gigantic waterfall that thundered down from the heights above. There was little hope of getting across the furious whirlpool that roared and raved at the foot of the colossal torrent.

'We're going to have to climb the rocks alongside.' Dan looked apologetically at Sir Hubert and Digby. 'Think you can make it, sir? And you, Dig?'

'I'll make it,' said Sir Hubert, stoutly. 'Don't bother to ask Miss Peabody. I *know* she's tough enough.'

'I'll be okay, Colonel Dan,' grinned Digby. 'Just let me go first. Then, if I slip, one of you others can catch me.'

Dan nodded. 'But *dont*' slip, Dig! Honestly, you're a bit of a weight for anyone to field!'

Half way up the gruelling climb, they *had* to stop for a rest. Despite his lion's heart, Sir Hubert's age was telling on him. And even the stalwart Digby was puffing even more than usual. Dan fretted naturally at the delay – but his agitation was nothing compared to Sondar's. 'There will be pursuit, Colonel! They will have the zom – you would call it a kind of dog – upon our scent!'

And Sondar was absolutely right . . .

*

Close – so close behind them, Treen guards had found the paralysed monster near the jetcopter wreck. Worse, they had found a Space Fleet jacket. For Digby, in the heat of the jungle, had unthinkingly taken it off and – tired of his captain's rank – discarded it along with his cap!

'It is the one the fat human was wearing,' said a Treen. 'Excellent.' Another came forward with a savage, vulpine animal with twin tusks, like those of a rhino, on its snout. 'Give it here, so that the zom may sniff it! We'll have them . . . and very soon!'

The friends had continued their climb. They were fairly close to the summit of the waterfall when luck, for a moment, seemed to turn their way. It was Sondar who found the plants that he knew would serve to give his human companions nourishment. 'Come – the leaves, the roots – the fruits on the branches. Eat them! They are rich in the substances you need!'

Dan had taken him at his word, and at his example, the others had munched eagerly. 'Hey, this isn't bad grub at all!' Digby's beaming face became animated with delight. 'Not up to the standards of my Auntie Anastasia's cooking, of course – but very acceptible under the . . . under the . . . ' His voice tailed off!

'What's wrong, Dig?'

'Oh, no, Colonel Dan! Down there – look!' The tubby batman's face lost its humour, and as they followed the pointing finger, the others saw why! There, at the foot of the waterfall, was the party of Treen guards, clambering up onto the lowermost rocks, their agile zom scrabbling before them!

'Confound them all!' Dan urged his companions on and up the last stretch of the climb. 'Get moving! There's only a couple of dozen feet to go, and maybe we'll have a clear run!'

Their breath rasping in their lungs, they hurled themselves upwards, fingers tearing at the ragged stones. Gratefully, they crawled over the last few feet and stayed, heads hung down, gulping huge draughts of air into their lungs. 'We – we made it, Dan!' Sir Hubert watched drops of his own sweat spattering down from his forehead, to be lost among the watersplash of the thundering falls on the flat rocks of the summit. 'We made it!'

But the silence of his companions made him look up. Instinctively, before his eyes left the ground, he knew they hadn't made it at all!

'Out of the frying pan . . . ' Digby's voice was just a half-heard whisper. For there in front of them, shoulder to shoulder, were at least a dozen Treen guards!

Typically, Dan didn't hesitate. Worn out though he was, he flung himself forward.

Conscious that Sondar was right beside him, that Sir Hubert, finding a new and desperate vitality, was yelling a rallying cry and firing his paralysing pistol into the enemy ranks, Dan used fists and feet in the incredible mêlée that erupted on the waterfall summit!

A Treen spun away from a knuckle-cracking blow, to

crash into one of his companions. And it had been Sondar who'd hit him! 'Attaboy!' yelled Dan. 'We'll see this through together, chum!' He lashed out and sent another opponent reeling!

But the odds were too great! Lancing rays from the weird helmets that the Treen guards wore cast solidifying bubbles of tough plastic, and Digby was first to be enclosed in one of these! Struggle though he might, he couldn't break loose. He was held totally captive!

Then it was Sondar's turn! Their plucky ally rolled inert!

Dan spun on his heel. He'd heard the snarling of the savage zom as it bounded over the lip of the drop behind him! The reinforcements – the pursuit that had driven them up and into the trap – had arrived!

As the animal leaped, Dan flipped over on his back and threw his knees up. The zom crashed to the dirt and lay still . . . Then he saw Jocelyn Peabody, on her knees, menaced by a Treen towering over her! Dan barrel-rolled and sprang to his feet. 'Look out, Prof! Behind you!'

The Treen stumbled . . . just as Sir Hubert, from the far side aimed a shot and fired. It clipped across the green Venusian's back, missed the girl by a fraction – and hit Dan squarely in the chest!

'Oh, *NO*!' Sir Hubert, appalled at what he had unwittingly done, threw himself between the two Treens who were racing for him and clutched wildly at Dan's staggering, paralysed

figure! His fingers found the front of Dan's jacket and clawed for a hold, but the stiffly teetering feet of the Colonel were back-pedalling towards the lip of the falls! 'Dan! *DAN*!' Sir Hubert's voice rose to a shrill yell as the inert, unseeing body hovered – poised for one frightful instant over the incredible drop!

And then it was too late. Without a sound, Dan arched backwards into space. Sickeningly, tumbling over and over, he fell away in dizzy perspective towards the boiling maelstrom of the whirlpools far, far below, and Sir Hubert Guest screwed his eyes shut so that he wouldn't have to witness the end.

CHAPTER NINE

## ENTER THE MEKON!

Sir Hubert was still there, stunned with the enormity of the disaster, when the sounds of struggle died away behind him and, easily and without haste, a Treen came up behind and enveloped him in one of the vast plastic prison bubbles. Professor Peabody, her gun knocked from her hand, had also been captured – but to Sir Hubert, nothing seemed to matter any more. The thought kept dinning through his mind . . . 'Dan is dead! Dan is dead!

Their Treen captors seemed in no way put out by the fracas that had taken place. The prison bubbles were carried between them across perhaps a mile of country. Then a waiting transporter vehicle took them to the terminal of the electrosender. Within ten minutes, they were back in Mekonta.

The Director of Research was there in his headquarters. Casually, he pointed to Professor Peabody. 'The woman first,' he snapped.

Obediently, a guard stepped forward and raised some kind of pistol! 'No! For pity's sake – don't!' Sir Hubert's high-pitched shout of horror came thinly through the envelope of plastic around him!

'Calm yourself, Sir Hubert! My assistant is merely about to

use his disintegron to cut through the bubble that imprisons her . . .'

Sure enough, the Treen's action was harmless, and soon the girl, Sir Hubert, Digby and Sondar were standing free.

'And now – I warn you not to attempt any further escape. It has been proved to you how futile your efforts are when compared with the power of the Treens!'

'They were not trying to escape, master.' Sondar was saying. 'There was an accident to the jetcopter. They were merely trying to find a way out of the jungle, with all its perils.'

'Good old Sondar,' thought Sir Hubert. 'He's keeping his word to us!'

There must have been times when the heat of the torrid forest had affected the central tele-scanner and made accurate observation diffficult, for the Director seemed to accept Sondar's explanation. With a gesture, he dismissed him, and their Treen ally strode silently from the chamber.

'And now – you three. I bid welcome to Mekonta to you, Sir Hubert, and to you, Professor Peabody. I am, of course, being sarcastic, in the manner so beloved of earthlings! But it may interest you to know that, for the present, the experiments on you are to be delayed.' He turned to Digby. 'You and your late lamented Colonel expressed a wish to see our Supreme Scientist – the Illustrious First One of Venus. Well, your wish has been granted. The Mekon' – he spoke the word reverently, his head inclining in a slight bow – 'has decreed that you shall be brought before him! He wishes to see for himself the puny aliens who have caused us so much trouble.'

The Director turned, and beckoned his prisoners to follow. 'We shall travel by telesender. And I warn you – attempt nothing with our magnificent leader. His powers are limitless, and he can see directly into your feeble minds!'

Sir Hubert managed to whisper an urgent message to his companions. 'If it's true, and he interrogates us, think and say the opposite to the truth!'

'I wonder what kind of a being this Mekon is,' breathed Digby. 'Probably some sort of walloping great giant with four heads and half a dozen arms on each side! I can't say I'm looking forward to the meeting!'

The telesender whipped them to a vast and spacious anteroom at one end of which there was a darkened niche – in almost total blackness.

'There's something in there,' muttered the girl. 'I can sense it!'

'It's hardly big enough to hold a giant,' said Digby.

And then, suddenly, the niche was flooded with light, and the three friends gasped in amazement as a tiny, floating platform the shape of half a walnut came cruising out towards them, hovering five feet or so from the floor. And seated on this astonishing vehicle was a small, spare individual with thin limbs and hands that trailed elongated, pointed fingers, His domed head, enormous in proportion to the size of his body, carried the severely reptilian features of the typical Treen – but his eyes were totally without expression, seeming to bore right into their souls!

'Behold! *The Mekon*!'

'You are wise to decide to collaborate and escape the useless fate of your headstrong colleague, Colonel Dare!' The voice was thin and high-pitched, and grated on the nerves.

'He comes straight to the point, doesn't he!' Digby was being brazen as usual. 'No "good evening, gentlemen", or anything like that! Proper rude, I call it!'

'The fat one is a fool.' The Mekon glared piercingly at Digby for one instant, then spun his aerial chair round to face one of a

series of huge, circular lens-like apertures that ranged along one wall.

'Come over here. I have to tell you that we are planning to reorganise your ridiculous planet. It is time that it was regularised and used to further the ends of science. *Our* science.'

One bony hand shot out, and as if by unseen command, the lens came alive, like a deep-set screen. The scene was instantly familiar!

'It's New York!'

'No,' corrected the Mekon. 'It is a full-size replica of the city you call New York. It has been built many earth miles from here, and the picture you see is being transmitted by long-range scanner. Observe what happens to it when we power-activate our *telezero beam* . . . '

The friends were unable to stop themselves flinching in reaction as, right in front of their eyes, the city erupted in a sequence of gigantic explosions that reduced the total area to smoking rubble in the wink of a second!

'You see,' The Mekon waved his hand again, and the screen went blank, 'By this means, among others, we shall overcome any misguided resistance. Then we shall reduce your surviving population to scientific limits.'

'Resistance? You'll find plenty, you fiend!' Sir Hubert couldn't keep the anger from his voice. But the Mekon was unimpressed.

'Nuclear weaponry? My dear Sir Hubert, we Treens have

specially protective suits that will enable our forces to walk unharmed through the very centre of an atomic explosion – no matter of what size!'

'I believe him, Sir Hubert!' Professor Peabody's face was deathly white.

Sir Hubert had recovered his calm. He gave Digby and the girl a quick, meaningful glance, and they remembered his whispered instructions on the way to meet the Mekon. 'Where do we come in?' he asked.

'We wish,' said the Mekon, 'to test the extreme limits of human resistance. Then we shall extract your brains for further study.'

'Oh. Er – well, of course, we'll be glad to help you if you tell us more of your plans.' Sir Hubert had a job thinking the words, let alone saying them! as for Digby, his face was a positive leer of painfully forced agreement! 'I can't think of anything nicer!'

Meanwhile, where the narrow cone at the bottom of the vortex below the waterfall sucked its way through shattered bedrock, the stiff body of Dan Dare was spun downwards with incredible force! He should have drowned – but such was the volume of air drawn down with the reeling torrent that a blanket of it actually surrounded him, held there by centrifugal force!

There was no possibility of resisting the pull of the water – but Dan was conscious. And already he could feel the effects of the paralysing ray wearing off!

Battered and buffeted, he was turned round and expelled head-first in to clear water so suddenly that it was moments before he realised that he'd passed the lowermost suction-point of the terrifying whirlpool . . . moments before he realised that the surrounding blanket of life-giving air had gone!

Gasping, he shot upwards like a cork, to find himself bobbing on the troubled surface of an underground river, surging its way through a cavern whose walls were coated with an eerie, subterranean luminescence!

It took all Dan's waning strength to fight the swift current and swim his way to the nearer bank . . . but he made it. For long moments he lay inert. Then he picked himself up and began to stumble forward. He'd no idea where he was going – but some sixth sense seemed to be urging him on.

How long he staggered on his way, he could scarcely recall, but at long long last he felt the breath of a wind on his face! Could it be that he was approaching the surface of the planet?

Yes! There ahead – a shaft of daylight! Dan's spirits rose, and he found a new lease of strength.

Dan emerged cautiously, keeping low to the ground. But there was only silence to greet him. Carefully, he raised his head from the shelter of some rocks – then ducked back. Not two miles away, he could see the towering buildings of a city!

Again he looked. No – it wasn't Mekonta. In fact, it bore no resemblance to anything he'd seen in the Treen capital. Could it be some citadel of the blue-skinned ones he'd met when he and Digby first landed? Well, there was nothing to be gained by staying put!

Dan began to walk towards the place, expecting at any moment to be challenged. Yet though he drew nearer and nearer, there was nothing in the way of a living being to be seen.

Now he was among the first buildings. Certainly there was noise. The din of machinery going at full blast on all sides. But still no people!

Taking his courage squarely in both hands, Dan entered one of the buildings. To his amazement, he found himself in what seemed to be some kind of remotely controlled dairy! There were goat-like animals munching conveyor-supplied fodder – moving obediently to machines that milked them – returning to their food . . .

'What on earth?'

Emerging again, Dan chose one building with a huge tower on top of it. 'Best thing I can do is climb to the top and take a panoramic look round. This is all different to anything I've seen on this crazy planet so far!'

Once at his vantage point, Dan whistled in amazement. On the far side of the city he could see rolling, cultivated fields – as far as the horizon! Acre upon acre of standing crops – and in amongst them, the shining, articulated body of some kind of harvester!

'Maybe I *did* die! Maybe this is heaven! No, get a grip on yourself, Danny my boy! I suppose I'd just better keep pushing my luck and go down for a closer look at that harvester. Surely there'll be someone in charge of it!'

In about half-an-hour, Dan had approached to within hailing distance of the appliance. It was big. Very big. But once again, it had no apparent driver. Dan stood looking at it, his hands on his hips. It stopped, and its reaping equipment was drawn in. It seemed to have finished its work.

Trotting, Dan moved in the wake of the huge harvester, which eventually halted beside a series of unloading cranes – each fully automatic – that took the ready-baled crops and piled them, one after the other, on an interminable moving highway that wound over the landscape until it disappeared into the hazy distance.

'In for a penny, in for a pound,' muttered Dan, clambering up on to the nearest bale. 'Wherever it's going, I'm going, too.' He settled down and relaxed.

Fatigue at last overcame him. That and the warmth of the Venusian day. And lulled by the peaceful progress of the smoothly-flowing conveyor highway, Dan slept.

He awoke suddenly. And with a yell of alarm! For one instant, he wondered what was happening to him, for steel arms had clamped around him, hoisting him upright – shaking him like a dog! He struggled madly before he realised that he must have reached the end of the moving highway – that his particular bale was being mechanically unloaded, and him with it!

'*Urrrgh*!' Unceremoniously, he was dumped down, the bale was split open, and in a shower of loose straw, he landed in

nothing less than a manger! He knew it was a manger, because the head of an animal very much like a cow dipped through a hatch towards him, ready to munch!

'Good grief!' yelped Dan – and the animal, its eyes wide, drew back and bolted!

Stiffly, Dan struggled out into what was clearly an open byre. Other animals – now that he could see them, they were more like a cross between cattle and horses – stared dumbly at him.

And then came the voice.

'Hey, Mac! What's cooking?'

'Uhhhh?' Dan spun round, to see a diminutive boy, brown-skinned, with a mop of fair hair, grinning cheekily up at him.

'Got any gum, chum?' said the kid.

Dan found his speech with an effort. 'Who taught you that?' he croaked. 'Come on – *who taught you*?' An incredible, impossible hope had set his heart hammering within his chest!

'Come on, earthman! I'll take you to him!' Cheerfully, the boy grabbed the astonished Colonel by the hand.

It could hardly have taken longer than ten minutes before they reached a thick grove of trees – lush, fruit-bearing trees. But to Dan it had seemed like hours! And from somewhere within the grove, he could hear the nasal twang of a voice lifted in song . . . an unmistakable American voice, underpinned and harmonised by a bass in lilting French accents!

'Pierre! Hank! It – but it just *can't* be!'

The song died away as Dan burst through the trees, ahead of

the boy. Two familiar faces were staring at him. Their expressions went through a comical variety of changes . . . amazement, suspicion, realisation and delight! And then –

'Dan, boy! Jiminy, by all that's wonderful!' Hank was wringing his hand with an intensity that threatened to tear it off. 'Mon brave! Mon vieux! Mon ami!' Pierre capered like a ten-year-old, his chubby face beaming, his expressive arms windmilling! 'How did you get here? Where are the others?'

'I thought you two were dead!'

The boy who had met him came up with a cup of some refreshing liquid.

'Thanks, sonny. That's better.' Dan wiped his lips. 'The others are prisoners in a place called Mekonta,' he said. 'I'm pretty certain they're alive. All of them . . . '

'But the Treens captured your comrades, eh, Colonel?' A new voice came in, and Dan turned to face the tall, kindly-looking man who was at his side.

'Oh, sorry, Dan.' This was Hank. 'Let me introduce Volstar. He's one of our hosts – the Therons. They're swell guys, all of them!'

'We had despaired of you, Colonel – knowing that you had landed in the northern hemisphere of our planet . . . ' Volstar returned Dan's hand-shake of greeting.

'You know our green friends, then . . . '

Volstar was joined by other Therons. They all looked very much alike. Handsome – well-shaped, with alert, mobile faces.

'Only too well, although our two civilisations have had no direct contact for centuries. Thanks to the flame-belt.'

'But you are tired, Colonel,' put in another. 'First, you must rest and refresh yourself. Then we will tell you our story.'

Dan shook his head. 'No. I've got to get the others out of Mekonta. Fast.'

'That's almost impossible, colonel. There is no way through the flame-belt, and the Treens maintain an aerial rayfield above it to prevent anyone flying over. The only faint hope is that we might be able to negoitate. By radio.'

'Negotiate? I didn't sign any pacts to get through the flame-belt – but I'm here!' Dan rubbed his chin. 'I swam. Through a subterranean river!'

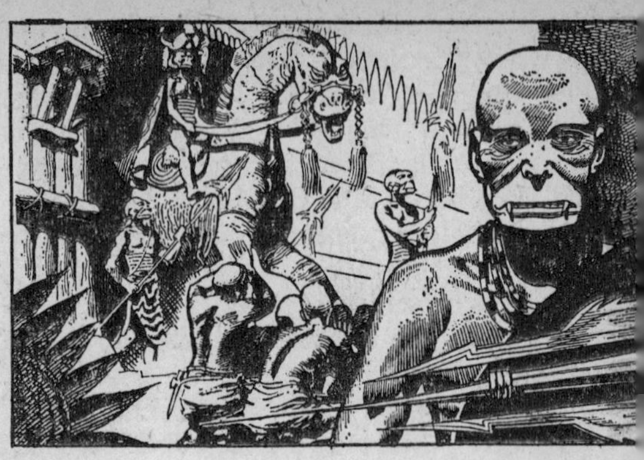

The Therons were amazed! 'Incredible! You mean there's a river from the north? Right under . . . ?'

'Exactly,' said Dan. 'Look. You're obviously friendly towards us. In a nutshell, we're here in the hope of making arrangements of food for our people on Earth. A matter for discussion with your President, I'd say. So I've got to see him. Maybe he'll be able to help us with a rescue attempt as well . . . '

'Dan.' Pierre clutched at his Colonel's sleeve. 'Before you go on. The Therons are helping us rebuild our rocketship. They have wonderful technology, Mon ami.'

'Great,' said Dan. 'And . . . ?'

'We have to contact Earth, Dan,' continued the French Canadian. 'You see, the Therons have told us about the Treens and their "earth plan".'

'Earth plan?' Dan looked puzzled. 'That's a new one on me!'

Volstar laid his hand on Dan's shoulder. 'They have long been making preparations to conquer your planet, Colonel. Really – I must insist that you are given the full facts before you do *anything*.'

It was all too much. Dan found himself scowling with concentration as he tried to absorb all the implications of what they had said. What was happening to him? He'd been able to sleep, hadn't he? And then his surroundings seemed to dissolve in a dizzy whirl, and he slumped forward to the ground, his last conscious registration the cries of alarm from his friends.

CHAPTER TEN

# COLOUR ME BLUE

It had been the result of accumulated strain. But now, thanks to the sophisticated doctoring of the Therons, Dan Dare awoke feeling fitter than he'd ever felt before.

The first person he saw was Volstar, who welcomed him warmly back to the land of the living.

'Is it my imagination, or are we moving?' Dan got up from an incredibly comfortable couch and looked around him. He was in a circular room, soothingly decorated, with plants growing in tastefully placed containers. 'Your house?'

'Yes, it is my house, and yes, we are moving,' said Volstar. Moving at about eight hundred of your earth miles per hour.'

'Jumping jets!' Dan ran to a nearby window.

'There is no slipstream because we are surrounded by a bubble of static air which travels with us. Now – we will join your companions, and you will hear something of the history of Venus – and of the Treens . . . '

Dan followed Volstar to a spacious living area where Hank and Pierre were waiting for him with some of Volstar's friends. There was discreet control equipment there that clearly guided the astounding flying house. That, and a bank of video-screens.

It was on these screens that Volstar drew up pictures to illustrate his – for want of a better word – lecture. From some sort of computerised memory bank, they told the story graphically enough!

'Venus has always been split in two by the flame-belt,' Volstar began. 'But the development of the two halves has always been different. Aeons ago, we in the south had developed a science more advanced than the Earth has now. But in the north a barbarous, brutal and reptilian race had evolved. About one hundred thousand years ago, we built aircraft with refrigerated cabins to cross the flame-belt and explore the north. When we landed, the Treens attacked us with giant reptiles . . .'

Volstar paused as his guests shook their heads at the scenes of violence.

'Finally, we triumphed,' he went on. 'We taught the Treens all we knew – but they cared only for revenge, and power. Machines became their masters, so we left them to their own devices . . .'

'But you still have machines,' interrupted Dan. 'This house . . . your factories . . . the mechanical roads . . .'

'Quite,' smiled Volstar. 'But machines work for us. We are not *their* slaves.'

'Let him go on, Dan.' Characteristically, Pierre was impatient.

'Well,' said Volstar. 'You may be astonished to know that we – having studied the planet for a long time – made an expedition to Earth. We were greeted in friendship by the high

priests of the Sun-God religion at that time practised by your civilisation . . . a civilisation, if you'll pardon me, that you know little about, despite the efforts of your archeologists.

'However, unknown to us, the Treens had followed us in space ships of their own. Unlike us, they had not come in friendship – and they attacked. There was much slaughter. They took many captives. The site of their treacherous assault was called – Atlantis!'

Dan and the others looked at each other in amazement. So *this* was the secret of Atlantis!

'Go on, Volstar . . . '

'The Treens made off unscathed – but the fury of the Atlantine revenge was turned on us. A ship or two escaped – but one was damaged by an Atlantine who had no knowledge of what he was doing. Its atomic engines exploded – and the whole centre of Earth's civilisation was destroyed, to sink beneath the ocean for ever! And that' – Volstar switched off the screen – 'is our story'. He sat back. 'You cannot wonder why we decided not to interfere with Earth again!'

Dan cleared his throat. 'Those blue characters. Up in the north. Are they descendants of the Treens' captives? The last Atlantines?'

Volstar nodded. 'Yes. The Venusian atmosphere has altered the pigment of their skin over the centuries, and they have developed deformed foreheads. And, of course, they continue to be slaves of the Treens.'

One of Volstar's friends had come up, waiting respectfully for silence. Now he broke in. 'We are approaching our destination, Volstar. Our guests had better make ready for their meeting with our president.'

'Ahoy there, Volstar!' The booming voice came from outside, somewhere. 'Is Colonel Dare aboard?'

'It is a guardship,' explained Volstar. 'It will take you to our president's house. As we all do, he lives in such a dwelling as this. We find we have no need of cities – although we maintain them as remotely controlled factory areas, as you have already seen.'

Dan – his uniform had been made as good as new since his arrival in Volstar's house – was taken aboard the guardship along with Hank and Pierre. It wasn't long before they were guided to the presence of the Theron President, an elderly man, wise of face, who was sitting relaxed in the patio garden of his home, surrounded by his family. He greeted the newcomers warmly.

'We are both interested and disturbed by the information you have brought from Treenland, Colonel Dare. I understand that you wish to ask my help in returning for rescue?'

'That's so, sir. You've been told about the underground river, of course.'

The President inclined his head. 'Listen, Colonel. Since their defeat, the Treens' fear of us has kept our races apart. That is good. We Therons have achieved a balanced life – we are free to pursue what is good and beautiful. We have found happiness, and we wish to keep it that way – for our children.' He reached down and gently ruffled the hair of one of his grandsons.

'Can you be happy knowing that the Treens are always a threat, sir?' Dan spoke persuasively. 'Can you be happy knowing that my people on Earth are in danger of starving?'

The President waved a hand emphatically. 'I am willing to help with the food situation, Colonel . . . '

'No, sir – please let me finish! The Treens are planning a conquest of my planet! What use will food be if those fiends gain the upper hand? And then – will their lust for power cease? No! Despite their fear of you, they'll want this southern hemisphere for their own!'

Hank and Pierre hardly dared breathe. Their eyes were on the President, clearly troubled by Dan's eloquence.

'Sir!' The Colonel pressed home his advantage. 'Think of it! That little boy, there! Is he to grow up facing the threat of a massive Treen invasion? And just because you and your contemporaries, in your happiness, have seen fit to bury your heads in the sand and ignore what's going on around you?' Dan shook his head and turned away.

'Colonel Dare.' A silence had fallen on the garden, but now it was broken as the President reached out for Dan's arm. 'Forgive me. You have shamed an old man. I see that the Earth still has something to teach us, and I give you my word here and now. We will help!'

The faces of the three space fleet pilots broke out into smiles of utter relief. Dan shot his hand out to grip the President's. 'Thank you, sir. Thank you from the bottom of my heart!'

The four of them – Dan, Hank, Pierre and the President – had been long in conference in the President's office. His inner sanctum. His explanations of Theron technology had given Dan the germ of a plan.

'We have three objectives, sir,' he said. 'First, Pierre and Hank must return in their repaired rocketship to Earth, and give them warning of what's happening here. Second, I must return to Mekonta and rescue our friends. Third, we all have to put our backs into defeating the Treens' ambitions for conquest. Let's take my part first. I use the word disguise, but I think,

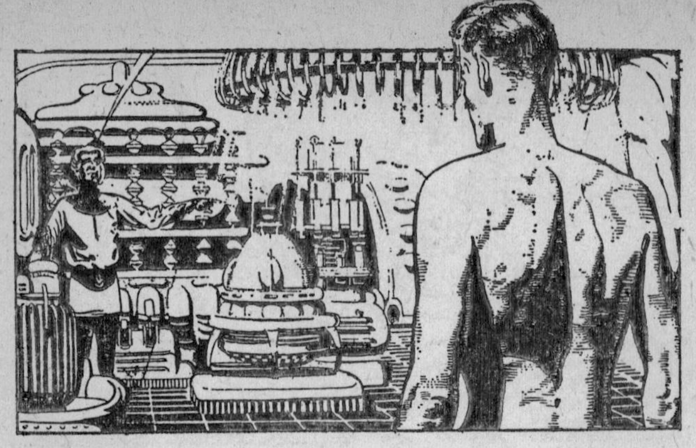

with the facilities available, it'll be better than that – but can you fix me up to look like an Atlantine?'

'Dan!' Pierre was shocked. 'You want to turn blue?'

'It's elementary, Pierre! The only way I'm going to pass unnoticed in the north is if I look part of the scenery.' He turned to the President again. 'How about it, sir?'

'It can be done – fairly easily. Your skin can be coloured. A wig can be made to give you Atlantine hair – the characteristic forehead bump can be built into it. And also' – the President chuckled – 'a device can be built into that wig which will allow you to speak and understand the language that is peculiar to the Atlantines!'

'You ain't kiddin', sir?' Hank uncrossed his long legs and looked doubtful. 'I mean – you can really turn Dan into a livin' replica of one o' these blue babies?'

'Come. See for yourself!' The President led the way to ante-chamber where a curious device almost like a giant sun-ray lamp hung down from the ceiling. 'Stand under that, Colonel Dare, while I switch on. Now. *Think* of an Atlantine . . . '

It was uncanny! One moment, Dan's face was its normal flesh colour. Then it became blue. Then, as the President switched off, it returned to normal. 'The effect can be as permanent as we desire,' he smiled.

'So let's make it permanent as of now,' said Dan. 'I'm thinking again!' The switch clicked over, and this time, Dan stepped from beneath the machine – apart from the wig that

would shortly come – a perfect replica of one of the Treens' slave race!

'And what now, mon blue-skinned colonel?' Pierre was overawed.

'What now? Why – we've got to drum up some transport that'll take me through that underground river – mon brave!' Dan grinned hugely. 'I've no intention of swimming my way back, and that's for sure!'

'This we can do as well,' said the President. We will journey to our old capital, where you will witness what I promise to be – for you – an almost miraculous feat of construction. 'I'm sorry,' he added apologetically. 'I often become smug at the triumphs of Theron science!'

'Smugness I can take,' said Dan. 'You show a proper pride in your achievements. Not like the Treens! They just take it as part of their born right!'

The President called a colleague and gave orders for the manufacture of Dan's Atlantine wig. Then he called for a guardship, and the four of them set off on a northward course towards the area where Dan had surfaccd from the underground river. 'I'd like to take a closer look at it,' the President explained. 'So that I can have the full requirements for a suitable craft at my fingertips, so to speak.'

CHAPTER ELEVEN

## GONE FOR A SOLDIER

The Treens in the central research laboratories of Mekonta were unusually quiet. The Director himself, used to uttering arrogant commands, was cringing under the steely gaze of the tiny, dome-headed figure surveying him so bleakly from the hover-platform above.

The face may not have shown it, but the Mekon was displeased!

'These earthlings,' he snapped. 'It is obvious from their evasive answers to our questions that they are not co-operating! They speak in riddles. They utter gibberish. They make statements we know to be false. They are deliberately resisting our examination!'

'Can it be that their minds are better than we imagined, Mekon? I mean . . . ' The Director's voice withered away under the glare of those baleful eyes.

'Fool! Their intelligence is nothing compared with ours! Where are they now?'

'In the isolation room, Mekon! They have been there for twenty-four of their earth hours! I wished to see whether, cut off from all contact with us, they began to break down!'

But if the Treens hoped that they were wearing down their

captives, they were unlucky. Sir Hubert, Digby and Professor Jocelyn Peabody were made of sterner stuff!

'Do you think we've managed to fool them, sir?' The girl raised her chin from her hand.

'Oh, I doubt it. We've fed them some pretty rum information. They'll have the dickens of a job sorting it all out.' Sir Hubert smiled at a recollection. 'Your long discourse on Wigan and your aunt Anastasia was a masterpiece, Digby.'

'I thought so myself, sir,' said Digby without modesty. 'Dunno what the old lady would say if she knew I'd told a green-faced wonder she was a top scientist, with the secret of converting black puddens' into miniature spacecraft!'

'What do you suppose they're doing back home?' mused Professor Peabody. 'I suppose they'll have given us up for lost, and recalled the mother ship.'

'I wouldn't be surprised, my dear. It's a little much to hope that *Ranger*'s still circling Venus, waiting for news of us, anyhow. What *I'd* like to know is how far the Treens have got with their plans to invade. My blood runs cold at the thought of these evil monsters roaming over our planet. I only hope we'll get a chance to put a spoke in their wheel – even if it means sacrificing ourselves in the attempt!' He drew a long sigh. 'If only Dan weren't lost to us!'

Digby snorted, remembered himself, and looked apologetic. 'Sorry to contradict you, sir ' he said. 'But beggin' your pardon, I don't reckon Colonel Dan's dead at all! I've been with him through thick an' thin, sir . . . and I won't believe he's gone until I'm standin' by his graveside!' The tubby batman glared down at the floor. He didn't see Sir Hubert shake his head, sadly . . .

The guardship, on hover behind them, had set down Dan, Hank, Pierre and a party of Therons led by their President by the entrance to the underground river. They could hear the torrent rushing, far below.

'It's about a fifty foot drop,' said Dan. 'Any chance of having this outlet enlarged?'

The President turned to one of his aides. 'Bring up a party of constructor robots. Open the cave and make a slipway capable of taking a craft up to thirteen tubits weight!' The President scrambled past Dan to look down into the faint luminescence of the void. 'Yes. I have it. Come, Colonel Dare – we have seen enough. Now for your conveyance.'

'A submarine of some sort, Mr President?' Hank blinked through his glasses.

'Just so. And the factories at our abandoned capital will turn it out in less time than it takes to tell. Back to the guardship, gentlemen.'

Dan and his friends were soon flying over the city – the deserted city he well remembered. The sound of the constantly thundering machines, automatically operated, drifted up as they came in to land. 'Electronic brains look after these installations,' explained the President.

The President led the way to a vast building which he told them was devoted to the manufacture of water craft. 'Purely for pleasure purposes, these days,' he explained.

With Dan, he approached the complexity of a mass of electronic machinery which he called 'the master brain'. He spoke into a grid. 'You will jettison present task. Clear drafting selectors for new design! Submarine craft . . . '

Dan watched in fascination as the President reeled off the requirements.

'Overall length, not more than seven swades! Capacity, four people. Electronic pilot and radar-guide net for cavern navigation. No breathing apparatus or anything to show on the

surface. Secrecy of operation vital!'

'Is that it?' Dan spread his hands.

'That's it. The machine will be constructed in about ten earth hours.'

Next on Dan's list, the fitting of the wig that would make him into an Atlantine. At a signal that it was ready, the guard-ship took them back to the President's home. Dan slipped the thing over his head.

'It sure don't look much in the way of comfort,' Hank commented.

Dan looked at him blankly. He said: 'Banee Irtum inscruss banee umsa banee!'

'*Whaaat?*'

'It's all right,' laughed the President. 'The device is working perfectly! You see, he speaks and understands only Atlantine now! He's the real thing!'

'Dan, mon brave! Don't play games! He's kidding, no?' Pierre shook the Colonel's shoulders frantically.

But Dan only shrugged and gaped – until one of the Therons, grinning, reached up and took the wig from his head.

'Miraculous,' said Dan. 'Absolutely fantastic!'

'Give it to me for a moment,' laughed Pierre, clapping the wig on his own head.

'I reckon I'll pass,' said Dan as he took the wig back, cradling it in his hands.

'Just one more thing, Colonel Dare.' The President gave him

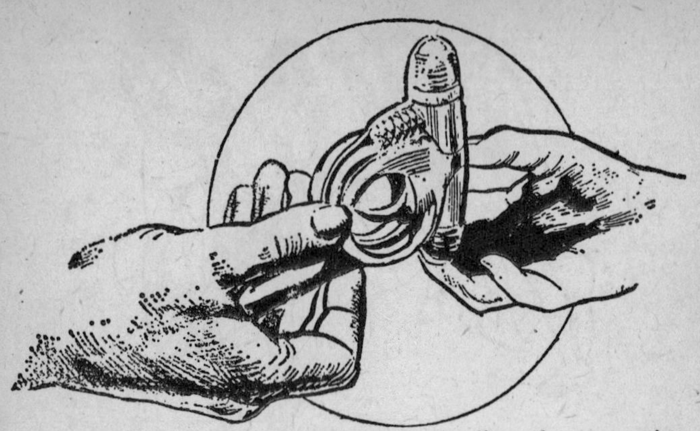

a small device. 'This tiny gadget neutralises the magnetism which is one of the Treens' chief sources of power. In an emergency, you may need it.'

It wasn't long before a Theron messenger arrived to report that rocketship Three – the vessel which had brought Hank and Pierre to Venus – had been repaired, and was now ready for re-launch. It was time for Dan to say au revoir to his two friends.

The farewells were necessarily brief. Old campaigners like these had been through too much together to waste mere words.

'Good luck, lads. And keep your fingers crossed for me!'

'The luck must be yours, Dan! Bon chance, mon Colonel!'

'So long, buddy. Oh yeah – and when you get that Professor Peabody clear, tell her to save a date for me. I thought she was kinda cute!'

Hank and Pierre left Dan to await the completion of his submarine. With a Theron escort, they were taken to a prepared launchsite outside the capital city. And there was their ship. As good as new. No, better.

'Should anything go wrong,' one of the Therons told them, 'We have fitted a homing device. It will bring you straight back here.'

Space suits had been provided, and the two men climbed into them. Then they were aboard, and with the minimum of fuss, the mighty rocket engines at the tail of the ship blasted into life!

Would *Ranger* still be up there, waiting for them? Or would they have to try and make it solo – over the long journey back to their home planet . . . ?

In the time it had taken Hank and Pierre to become space-borne again, Dan had taken delivery, so to speak, of his submarine. Robots had enlarged the entrance to the underground river, and now the sleek vessel was poised to go! A quick handclasp with the President, and Dan, wearing breathing equipment over his blue body – a necessity in case of emergency – settled in beside a strange box of tricks bearing the legend 'electronic pilot'. In keeping with tradition, Dan immediately christened him 'George'.

The sub sped down the inclined slope and plunged into the water. Dan sat back and relaxed. Clearly, with such a device as George skippering the machine, he didn't have to do a thing, except feed it verbal instructions which it deciphered and converted to obedient manoeuvres.

So far, it was easy. Too easy! Suddenly, in the clearness or of the luminously-lit water ahead, Dan saw a vague stirring that resolved itself into a writhing shape!

'Oh, oh! Company! We must be getting near the underside of the flame-belt, George . . . this is an aquatic relation of the monsters in the surface jungles!'

It was some kind of giant octopus – and it came questing for

the approaching craft, its enormous tentacles raised to clutch and kill!

'Give it the works, George! I know I can depend on you!'

At Dan's command, a sizzling blast of energy shot from the nose of the submarine!

The creature fell away, and the submarine cruised serenely through. And though Dan kept his eyes constantly peeled, there were no more incidents before the dials on his instruments told him that they had come through the south-north tunnel. That they were out in the open – in the hemisphere ruled by the Treens!

Gently, Dan ordered the auto-pilot to surface. It was night-time, and everything was deathly quiet as he bade a flippant farewell to George. 'Don't do anything rash,' he said. 'Just wait here. I hope – oh, how I hope we'll meet again, and I'll have my chums with me!'

Dan stepped ashore. In the distance, he could see lights – lights of what the Theron President had told him was likely to be an Atlantine village. Grimly, he made sure his wig was secure, and strode forward to test his disguise to the ultimate limit.

There was one vital factor that Dan didn't know. *Couldn't* have known! It had happened shortly after the launch of the reconstructed rocketship. The Treens had picked up the vessel on

their long-range scanners, and a report had gone straight to the Mekon! With no clear idea of what it meant, the fiendish little leader of the Treens had ordered the launch of interceptor ships, and now these were streaking in pursuit of Hank and Pierre!

It was Hank who saw them first. His eyes glued to the scanner screen on which he'd hoped to find the comforting blip of *Ranger* – he didn't know that *Ranger* had indeed been recalled to Earth – he saw the rapidly approaching enemy craft!

'I've got a contact, Pierre – but it isn't what we want! Pull 'em in on video!'

'Ma foi! Trouble! Hold on, Hank!'

Knowing that their small vessel was no match for armed battle craft, Pierre turned his controls to streak back for the safety of the southern hemisphere. And then the frail ship rocked and shuddered as a bolt of blasting power shot from one of the Treen attackers to burst alongside!

'Zut! We are out of control!'

'Jumpin' snakes! They're comin' in for the kill, Pierre.'

'Wait!' The Canadian darted his hand towards a switch on the panel before him. 'The homing device! It's our only chance!'

Miraculously, the stricken ship righted itself. A Treen attacker came boring in . . . then exploded violently as it struck some kind of force-shield the homing device incorporated!

Another met the same fate, moments afterwards, and a third turned tail for home! Shaken to the core, Hank and Pierre unwound and let their homer keep control. 'I sure hope Dan

has more luck with his end of the mission, pal! I'm afraid we've just drawn a great big blank!'

'Hey, mon ami.' Pierre looked grave. 'The Mekon – this leader of the Treens. Now he must know something is up, oui? What do you think he's going to do?'

'He'll figure two of his ships have been destroyed by a spacecraft from the southern hemisphere,' said Hank blandly. 'If I were him, I'd declare war!'

Pierre threw up his hands in despair. 'Of course he will! And among his forces – he'll use his slaves, no? The Atlantines! And who is going to be among the Atlantines when call-up comes? Dan! Sacre bleu, Hank – he'll be drafted into the Treen army!'

CHAPTER TWELVE

# KARGAZ, THE MIGHTY ONE!

A fire blazed in the hut at the centre of the Atlantine village. On a raised platform, the head man and his advisers faced a congregation of their blue-skinned fellows, and the mood was one of savage discontent!

The din of the shouting carried clearly to Dan Dare's ears as he approached through the gloom of the outskirts. Despite the translator in his wig, he could make nothing out in the confusion of voices – until suddenly, everything was still and silent.

In the hut, a young, sturdy Atlantine had roughly shouldered Ur-Tag, the head man, aside. Now his voice, and his alone, quelled the mob!

'Ur-Tag grows old! His blood is thin! This is a time for action – for young men to decide! In a few hours the Treens will be here to take us for their army . . . ' The orator paused, to glare meaningfully around the assembly. 'Why should our men die for them in their quarrel with those of the southern hemisphere? *We* have no fight with those they call the Therons! We have been slaves to the Treens long enough! I say we should resist!'

Outside, Dan stood stock still with amazement. 'My stars,' he breathed. 'War? The Treens and the Therons? What the blazes can have happened?'

Now the head man was speaking again. 'Do not listen to him, my children! It is useless for us to defy our masters! They have the power to crush us – to bring untold misery on our children for generations to come! They leave us alone as long as we continue to serve them – let us bow once more to their will!'

The younger man elbowed him aside again. 'We have no machines! No sophisticated weapons! But we have our strength! Our *will*! Let us fight them hand to hand! Let us die, rather than remain their vassals!'

'You're right, young man!' A hundred faces swept round to stare in amazement as Dan Dare strode through the doorway.

'You speak words of wisdom beyond your years!'

'A stranger!'

'Who is he?'

'He is not of this village!'

Ur-Tag came forward. 'Who are you, unknown one, that you sneak into my homestead like a lizard in the night?'

'I am a hunter . . . I have wandered.' Dan tried to keep up his commanding presence.

'But from which village? Speak, man! And where is your spear? Why did you not blow the horn of warning at the entrance gate?'

Inwardly, Dan cursed his own impetuosity. He'd scented the air of revolt, and had rushed willy-nilly into a situation that had already got beyond itself. The Atlantines were no longer interested in the young rebel's harangue. All they were concentrating on now was him!

They crowded round him. Suspicious. Hostile. Dan felt the wall of the hut against his back.

'Speak, I say, *speak*!' Ur-Tag dealt Dan a blow with his fist that knocked him sideways . . . that dislodged the wig and sent it spinning to the floor!

'Aieeeee!' The shrill cry that went up chilled Dan to the marrow. 'Ye gods! This is it! My cover's *blown*!'

And then – astonishingly, Dan saw that, far from hurling themselves on him, the Atlantines had flung themselves prostrate before his feet! A wailing cry went up from them . . .

'KARGAZ! KARGAZ!'

'I'm sorry, chums,' said Dan shakily. 'I won't know what you're blithering about until I clap my headpiece back on!' He reached down, retrieved it, and put it in position, in time to face the awe-stricken head man, Ur-Tag, who held his hands up as if in fear!

'Kargaz! You have come back to us – as it is written! Kargaz the mighty!'

'Yes. It is I! Kargaz!' Dan bluffed madly, wondering what the performance was all about. Luckily, it was Ur-Tag himself who did the necessary explaining. Turning to his prostrate villagers, he began to intone . . .

'The hero of centuries ago! The only Atlantine who ever successfully defied the Treens! The outlaw who disappeared and swore to return to lead our race to freedom! He has lived, my children! He has *lived*! It is as our young man' – he gestured towards the rebellious orator, now picking himself cautiously to his feet along with his companions – 'it is as our young man said! Now is the time! Our deliverer has *arrived*!'

'How did you know me for Kargaz?' Dan had decided to play along with this unexpected turn of events.

'By your *forehead*,' said Ur-Tag. 'I see you use disguised hair – to keep you safe from Treens, no doubt – but you have no real bump there! You are of our ancestors' race, when our foreheads were smooth!'

'Friend, you don't know how right you are,' thought Dan.

But he kept it to himself. 'The point is, what do I do now? I can't think of leading this unarmed rabble against the Mekon's men!'

A knotty problem. But the decision was taken clean out of Dan's hands! At that very moment, a young Atlantine burst into the hut, his voice shrill with panic. 'The Treens! They're here! They're here!'

In that packed hut, there was nothing that anyone could do. The Atlantines may have looked to him for guidance, but Dan was as helpless as the rest as the Treens poured in! He could only shout for them not to resist – to wait – to bide their time. And then they were herded out. Each Atlantine male. Herded out under the menace of Treen guns and formed up to join a column of other blue-skinned men that had been brought on the march.

While Dan was being taken away to join the ranks of an Atlantine assault division, his friends in Mekonta were recovering from a series of exhausting tests through which the Director, at the Mekon's express command, had put them. They had been strained to the limits of endurance. They were exhausted. Worn out. And worse – all three of them had been dumped in a bare room that had the smell of death about it. As Digby put it. 'It's like a sort of dustbin, and we're the rubbish.'

'I'm very much afraid you're right, Digby,' said Sir Hubert Guest. 'The Mekon's got his data formulated, and from what we've overheard from the guards, he's up to his scrawny neck in some kind of war with characters on the far side of the planet.'

'At least it's occupying him so completely he's had to shelve his plans for invading Earth, Sir Hubert.' Jocelyn Peabody ran her hands wearily through her hair. 'I suppose that's something!'

'I'd like to know what they're going to do with us. Now that they've – er – finished.' Digby put his hands on his hips and swept his gaze round their bleak surroundings. Absolutely featureless, save for some slits, high in one of the walls. 'What d'you suppose they're for? Ventilation?'

Suddenly, a thin, yellow mist began to drift through the apertures!

'Ventilation?' Sir Hubert caught hold of the other two by the

shoulders and bodily hauled them to the floor. 'They're *gas* inlets! They're going to *poison* us!'

'The extermination programme is in operation, Mekon!' The Director stood at the side of his leader, gazing up at the baleful eyes. 'The earthlings are of no more use to us.'

'Good. What of the war? Report on our progress!'

'We have cancelled the barrier ray above the flame-belt, Mekon. Telezero beam projectors are ready for operation, and reconnaisance craft are flying towards the southern hemisphere. Reflector craft are alerted for take-off as soon as optimum positions have been decided.'

'Excellent. The telezeros were designed to destroy Earth cities – but no matter. They can be brought just as usefully to bear on the Therons. Provided . . . ' The Mekon paused, and his eyes were suddenly blank and thoughtful. 'Provided that the Therons do not have technology that is greater than ours.'

'Do you *doubt* our power?' The Director's voice had a definite edge to it.

'Of course not,' snapped the Mekon, testily. 'What *can* be greater than the power of the Treens?'

Privately, the Mekon had doubts. And they were well founded! From the automated Theron cities, incendiary rays had been activated.

Safely back in the southern half of Venus, Hank and Pierre had rejoined the President, and together watched the video screens as a flight of Treen reconnaissance craft, sweeping over the area above the flame-belt, and through skies that had once been protected by their own barrier force-field, droned towards them.

'You don't think Dan could be . . . ' muttered Hank.

'In one of those things? Don't be crazy, mon brave! He's likely to be a mere Atlantine infantryman! Whatever problems he's having, it isn't flying a sophisticated Treen plane!' Pierre turned to the President. 'They will not get through, m'sieur?'

'They will *not* get through.'

Scarcely were the words out of his mouth before the leading Treen vessel checked, staggered in the sky, then burst spectacularly into flames! Completely out of control, it dived down towards a barren stretch of no-man's land somewhere south of the flame-belt!

Another ship fell, and yet another! The flight commander reported back to the Mekon, still – incredibly – without any emotion in his voice.

'Hostile incendiary rays at strength index nine point five and increasing. Do we proceed or return?'

The Mekon thought deeply. 'Remain in area. Avoid contact with incendiary rays.' He paused, and turned to the Treens clustered around him. 'It is clear to me,' he said thinly, 'that we have been too complacent. The Therons have been warned, perhaps, of all we are doing. Maybe they have known all along, or maybe that prisoner we considered dead – Colonel Dare – has somehow got through to them. If so, then they will try to warn Earth . . . '

'That would explain the take-off of that rocketship, Mekon,' put in one of his aides.

'Precisely, fool! Do not interrupt me! Should they succeed in contacting Earth, they may try and enlist aid. It would be inconvenient, to say the least. We must launch our attack on that planet at once.'

'But Mekon!' Another Treen flapped his hands helplessly. 'That would mean fighting on two fronts! Is that wise?'

'And our plan for Earth means first setting up a telezero station on their moon,' put in the first aide. 'Mekon – from what we know of the prisoners' courage and determination, the earthlings will fight hard to stop us . . . even if we surprise them. Can we afford a battle like that while we are engaged with the Therons?'

'We shall dupe them,' said the Mekon. 'We shall fool the Earth into believing that *we* are the friendly ones on Venus. And we shall use our captives to prove it! Turn off the killing gas and and have them revived – at once!'

Gasping – half dead, Sir Hubert, Professor Peabody and Digby were dragged from their room and hauled to resuscitation machines – glad to be reprieved, but with no knowledge of the part they were to play in the Mekon's evil schemes!

CHAPTER THIRTEEN

# UNDER THE ENEMY'S NOSE!

'Hm. The old town hasn't changed a bit!' Dan Dare obediently followed the cowed Atlantines out of the electrosender that had sped them to Mekonta. There were hundreds of them here on this Venusian equivalent of a barrack square, herded in line by cursing, blue-skinned NCOs while impassive Treens looked on.

Dan found himself split up from Ur-Tag's villagers – and perhaps it was just as well. He didn't want them constantly pestering him to lead them in some form of revolt. Not now. Not at this particular moment. The less attention he drew to himself for the time being, the better.

But it just didn't work out that way! Along with a crowd of other conscripts, he was issued with helmet, breastplate and uniform, and his practised hands, used to buckles and straps, stood out against the general fumbling of the others!

'Hey, you! Come here!' The voice was a raucous bellow, the like of which Dan had often heard during his original training, so long, long ago on Earth!

'Oh, oh! A sergeant major if ever I saw one!'

His fierce moustaches bristling, the non-com drew himself up to his full height and glowered down at Dan.

'And what have we here, eh? *Stand to attention in front of your Cohort Dapon-In-Chief!* Come on, lad – out with it! You're no raw yokel from a reservation!'

Dan knew he was in a tight spot! 'Dare I trust him? Just how pro-Treen are these regular soldiers?' His brain raced frantically. Yet he knew he had little alternative. Mentally crossing his fingers, Dan raised his wig just enough to show the Dapon his smooth forehead. 'Look!' he said.

The man's eyes widened. 'By the rays of the sun-god!' he breathed. 'Kargaz! Can it be true?' He grabbed Dan cautiously by the arm and drew him aside to the scant shelter afforded by an overhang on the commissariat building. 'Keep quiet and come under here!'

'Will you help me?' Dan looked at him, his gaze level and

steady.

The Dapon nodded. 'To the last drop of my blood!' His fists clenched. 'I can't believe it! Kargaz in the flesh! At last! That I should live to . . . But enough! What are your orders?'

Dan decided that, as some kind of reincarnation of Kargaz the Mighty One, he could say what he liked to the Dapon and be believed – unquestioningly. He'd tell him that he had Earth friends here in Mekonta who must be rescued . . . that their freedom was essential for the Therons to win the war and vanquish the Treens. That with the Treens beaten, there would be a new freedom for the Atlantine race . . .

The Dapon listened, his face tightening with enthusiasm, his eyes gleaming. 'I think I know how this rescue can be done,' he said.

Sir Hubert Guest, Professor Peabody and Digby, now fully recovered, were once more in the presence of the Mekon. The evil little Venusian studied them carefully.

'You are lucky to be alive. But for my intervention, you would have died in great pain. But I am going to offer you an alternative to death. I wish you to pose for some pictures, and to record certain messages to my directions. Agree, and you will be spared and sent to work with the Atlantine convicts in the mines at the North Pole.'

'Phew,' said Digby. 'I'd smell a rat if *you* weren't so close, you little devil! You can't want pictures for your family album – a thing like you couldn't have a family!'

'Abuse will not anger me, fat one.'

Sir Hubert spoke up. 'Whatever your scheme is, it's bound to be bestial. We'll have nothing whatever to do with it, and that's absolutely final!'

The Mekon considered. 'Take them away. I will give them a little time to think over my offer. I cannot believe these fools would deliberately choose to die!'

When they had gone, the Mekon turned to his Research Director. 'I think they will eventually agree. The plan is this. We shall send a ship to Earth with pictures of the prisoners as though they were injured on landing, but are being looked after well in Mekonta. We shall say we are willing to help Earth with food, but that it is necessary – here we shall lie greatly – to build transfer stations on the Moon to change the ships' atmospheres from Venus air to Earth air. The earthlings will allow this – but we shall install telezero reflectors so that we can bombard the Earth into submission! Such conquest will be absurdly easy, and will leave our main resources to continue the task of crushing the Therons!'

It is a brilliant concept, Mekon,' intoned the Director.

Thanks to Dan's quick grasp of anything he was taught, it had taken him no time at all to learn the elementary Atlantine drill movements that the Dapon had taught him. A firm bond of friendship had quickly grown between these two. The Dapon called him Dan – to have publicly used the name Kargaz would have made the Treens highly suspicious. In return, Dan called the Dapon 'Handlebars' because of his luxuriant moustache.

Now Dan was in his place as part of the palace guard, personally led by the Dapon. They were about to effect a change-over with the existing squad, and the Dapon had assured Dan that his soldiers were hand-picked. Treen-haters to a man!

The Colonel had never felt so tense before. This was it! They'd received orders to assemble the prisoners and march them to the Mekon for their final ultimatum. At the back of the squad, he stood silent and rigid as the Mekon hovered above his captives.

'Have you come to your senses? Have you decided to co-operate?'

'No,' said Sir Hubert, flatly.

The Mekon turned unconcernedly, and his finger pointed straight at Dan. 'I can waste no further time. They will be killed one by one. First, the fat human. Guard – *shoot* him!'

Obediently, Dan swung his blast-rifle into the aim. But then he swivelled abruptly, and the charge that burst from the barrel smashed straight into the Treen leader's hover platform!

The domed head slammed sickeningly to the floor as the Mekon fell – and lay still! Not one of the gaping Treens in their master's throne room had made a move! Then the guns of the Dapon and his men were turned on them, and Dan stood astride the huddled, unconscious figure!

'One tricky move by any of you Treens, and I kill the Mekon!'

The three captives were staring at him in stupefied disbelief. He winked straight at Digby.

'It – it's Colonel Dan! He's talkin' gibberish, but it's *Colonel Dan!*'

Dan lifted his hand to disconnect the switch in his wig for a brief moment.

'Dead right, Dig! But this is no time for explanations! Just trust me!'

He swung round to the Dapon, even as he grabbed a fistful of the Mekon's skin and tucked the inert body under one arm . . .

'We need a ship! They won't touch us while we've got their top boy as hostage! Just show us the way!'

A quick burst of fire effectively paralysed the stunned Treens in the room. Then the four friends and their Atlantine allies were racing for the nearest Electrosender entry! Hurriedly they scrambled inside a car – but before the door closed, a lone Treen hurled himself in beside them!

The Dapon brought his gun into the aim!

'Stop!' said Dan. 'It's *Sondar!*'

'Take me with you!' Sondar was gasping for breath. 'They took me for analysis – discovered how I had helped you!

I managed to slip the guards in the confusion when you captured the Mekon!'

'Can we trust this man?' The Dapon looked highly doubtful.

'We can trust him, Handlebars,' grinned Dan. 'And come to think of it, he'll be able to fly our escape craft for us! Better than having to force the Mekon to do it. He's too tricky by half!'

There were armed Treen hoverbikes waiting as the electrosender delivered the fugitives to the main spaceport. But none of them dared fire for fear of hitting the Mekon. Dan knew they could never afford to destroy their supreme scientist!

'Which ship, Sondar?' Dan made no effort to conceal his hurry.

'That one!' Sondar pointed to a huge vessel, one of three standing in line against towering gantries. Each ship had a strange, almost arrow-shaped protrusion on its nose.

'What are they?'

'Telezero reflectors, Colonel Dare! All three are programmed to link up in space, so that the protrusions fit together to form a complete circle. The circle itself is like a mirror – to reflect the terrible telezero beam to its target!'

'Great! So removing one of them is going to spoil the set-up entirely. And I'll bet my boots the Therons will give their eye-teeth for a sample, delivered in good condition!'

There were personal hoverbikes at the electrosender terminal. At Sondar's instructions, the escapers mounted them. 'My thought-impulses are sufficient to get us across to the ship,' he said. 'Hold on!'

But then it happened! Dan had been confident that the Mekon, draped across his knees, was still unconscious . . . but the wily Venusian was nothing of the sort! As they passed over one of the canals, the Mekon kicked himself clear and dived to safety!

Instantly, all hell broke loose! Seeing their leader's escape, the hovering Treens opened up with everything they had! To his horror, Dan saw hoverchairs blown to pieces all around him!

'Hang on, Handlebars!' The Dapon's chair had been struck a glancing blow, but Dan's hand shot out to grab his falling ally in the nick of time! Then Dan remembered the device the Theron President had given him!

Hastily, he fumbled it out and pressed the switch. 'We're all going down! Us *and* the Treens,' he yelled! 'Happy landings – and head for that telezero ship!'

The friends were ready for it. The Treens were not! Their pursuit vehicles fell out of the skies as the device cancelled their magnetic power!

Breathless and dazed, Dan and his friends struggled to their feet. Only yards to go! It wouldn't be long before the opposition regrouped, and besides, Dan couldn't keep the device switched on once they were in their escape vessel!

One by one, they scrambled through the entry port. Dan. Sondar. Sir Hubert, Digby and Professor Peabody – miraculously still unscathed. The gasping Dapon and a pitiful few of his men . . .

'Take over, Sondar! Get this thing into the sky! Quickly!'

The engines roared into life – but outside, the enemy had re-formed! Now a shattering fussilade of fire blased the giant spaceship from all sides!

The Mekon, plucked from the water by his men, sat astride one of the attacking hovervehicles, and his voice came shrill and high over the din of firing!

'Conventional weapons will do nothing against the skin of the reflector ship! But it *must* not go to the Therons! They know nothing of this advance in our technology! Turn tele-

zeros three and seven on to this spaceport and fire maximum charge! Immediately!'

'But the *other* ships, Mekon – our people there!'

'Fool! Do you *question* my orders? You will die for such heresy!'

Within moments, the full savagery of the Treens' telezero weapons was unleashed! The sky bloomed with fantastic explosions as the entire structure of the spaceport was blown to smithereens! The refletor ships themselves, necessarily proofed against the beams they were designed to bounce, remained unharmed – but their gantries were toppling! The unmanned pair keeled over to smash heavily down on the shattered pads!

And yet – standing on its tail jets, blasting fire among fire – the third lifted clear! The Mekon's callous destruction had failed!

'We're away, Colonel Dare! We're *away*!' Sondar seemed to be making up for a lifetime of neglected emotion! His green face was positively beaming as he turned from the controls. 'They'll throw everything they have at us, and they could still cripple us by shooting out our engines. But we can fight! We *will* fight!'

'You're darned right we'll fight, Sondar! Just give us the instructions, and we'll obey! Where are the guns?' Dan mopped his brow. The strain had been immense – would still be immense. And to cap it all, he had to keep switching back and forth from Atlantine to open speech to make himself understood to the varied people there. It was likely that, by now, old Handlebars had tumbled to the fact that Dan wasn't Kargaz at all – but it didn't seem to matter any more. The Dapon's face was alight with the thrill of having dealt a bodyblow to the Treens and their infuriating sense of superiority.

The ship levelled out, far above the planet, and Sondar moved switches that exposed fighting turrets armed with long-range ray-guns. Dan lost no time in detailing his companions to man them. 'With your permission, Sir Hubert . . . '

'My boy, I'm under your command now! I've no idea how you've done all this, but it's been brilliant. Magnificent!'

'I told you he was never dead,' whooped Digby, forgetting the respect due his vastly superior officer.

Dan grinned. 'Come on, Prof. There's a double turret astern. We'll take it together.'

There was only one snag. A big one. Dan didn't know it, but even as he and his companions prepared to defend themselves from the Treens, danger was approaching from another, unexpected source. From the southern hemisphere, a wave of Theron fighters were zoning in to the attack!

For Theron monitors had recorded the launch of the telezero reflector – and telezero beams were something against which they had no definite defence! The order had gone out – 'destroy the ship at all costs!'

The brave assault swept northwards, towards the flame-belt over which the Treen ray barrier was still down. Below them, they saw the strewn wreckage of the reconnaisance craft that had been shot down. Ahead of them, somewhere, the giant target they were pledged to annihilate!

In that target, Dan and his friends were hard pressed. The Mekon, all other war plans temporarily shelved, had thrown everything he had after the telezero reflector. The concentrated might of his battle fleet had closed in on the fleeing vessel, and the skies were rent with unspeakable violence!

They came in from all sides, their guns blasting! Again and again the huge ship staggered under the impact of a hit!

Their guns hot in their hands, the defenders yelled defiance at the Treens. Digby was beside himself! 'Come on, you monkeys! Come and get the old Lancashire one-two!'

The Dapon – old Handlebars – pumped the triggers in his turret and roared defiance at the enemy he'd dreamed for so long of hammering!

Side by side, Dan and Professor Peabody saw the raking

effects of their fire send a Treen spinning away to its doom and exchanged a swift thumbs-up.

Sir Hubert snarled with the heat of an action he'd never expected to fight. Not at his age!

And still Sondar strove to control the huge craft, conscious of the grim-faced Atlantine gunners in the fire-pods beside him . . .

His face suddenly tensed. A light was blinking on a panel in front of him. 'Put on your oxygen masks! They have found a flaw in our plating! We are holed!' he yelled into the intercom.

In the same moment, shots from the enemy blasted into numbers one and two engine pods! The ram-jets died, and the reflectorship swung drunkenly off-course!

'Emergency! Emergency!' Sondar cut the remaining engine to stabilise the craft.

And then a chance shot from a Treen attacker struck home just behind the rearmost gunturret! Hurled against each other, Dan and Professor Peabody blacked out as their whole position sheared from the ship and tumbled out into free space! In the fraction of a second during which disaster had struck, the taste of victory had turned dismally sour!

It was just as though fate had turned its kindly face away. The telezero reflector hung motionless. A sitting target for the Treen survivors. And – horror piled upon horror – the attack wave of Theron ships were already in sight and boring home to add to the chaos!

## CHAPTER FOURTEEN

# SUPREME SACRIFICE

In the home of the Theron President, Hank Hogan and Pierre Lafayette listened fascinated to the incoming reports from the battle zone.

'We're going into the attack!' the crackling voice of the leader of the Theron assault flight was high with excitement!

'Give 'em beans, boys! Give 'em beans!'

Then . . .

'Wait! Attack leader to base! The Telezero reflector is already under bombardment . . . *from Treen ships!*'

'*Treen* ship?' The President shot out of his seat in incredulous amazement. 'But – but that is impossible!'

Pierre leaped up and grabbed the old man's arm. 'It's Dan!'

'What?'

'It's *Dan!* Don't you see, mon vieux? It *must* be! Why else would the green horrors attack their own ship if Dan hadn't captured it?'

'By Ramnas! You must be right!' The President whirled and stabbed his finger on the button of an intercom. 'Flight leader! Give all support to Telezero ship! We will send reinforcements!' He turned back to Hank and Pierre. 'What a chance for us! To get hold of such a vehicle as that – the Treens' most secret armament! Analysis would give us the means of building shield against their ultimate weapon! Gentlemen – I am joining our back-up forces! Will you come with me?'

'Just try and stop us!'

The two space-fleet pilots raced through the house after the President to the personal jet-car that would carry them to the so recently set up attack headquarters outside the capital city.

'Just you hang on, Danny boy,' yelled Hank. 'The cavalry's a-comin'!'

Brilliant flashes of light were exploding all around Dan and Professor Peabody. The integral gravity of their drifting turret allowed them to stand upright, but their eyes were full of despair as they saw the crippled telezero ship reel and reel again as the Treens slammed home their advantage!

'There's nothing . . . *nothing* we can do!'

'Oh, Dan! And look . . . *look!*' The girl pointed shakily out to where an enemy craft was streaking through the void, straight towards them! 'We're right in this one's sights!'

Then the miracle! Even as they tensed for the shock of oblivion, the Treen blew to fragments! Not from a despairing shot from the pitifully damaged telezero, but from a lancing burst of fire from a Theron fighter! Dan gasped as the shock-wave of gold-coloured avengers roared past, their guns blazing!

'By glory! As Hank would say, the cavalry's a-coming!' Dan was totally unaware that he'd repeated his old friend's very words! 'Now we'll see some action!'

'What do you mean, *now*? I've seen action enough to last me a lifetime,' said Jocelyn Peabody, weakly.

It was by no means over, though. The initial Theron onslaught caught the Treens on the hop, and craft after craft disintegrated in spectacular bursts of starfire. Yet the fighters from the southern hemisphere were still outnumbered, and retaliatory gunnery took its heavy toll! Dan clenched his fists as he saw one after another of the slim ships caught in Treenal crossfire!

'Not enough cavalry! Not *enough!*'

But here they were – the second wave! The big command

ship of the Theron President himself, and every available machine he'd managed to muster!

It was too much for the enemy. Shattered and shaken, their confidence gone, the remaining Treens turned their ships and streaked for home!

The Theron President's vessel cut engines and slid alongside the drifting turret. Within moments, Dan and Professor Peabody had safely been taken aboard, to hug Hank and Pierre in ecstatic reunion!

'Boy oh boy oh boy! Did we catch 'em! Man, it's good to see you again, ol' Danny – *and* you, Prof!'

'Parbleu! You escape by ze skin of ze teeth, mes braves!' Excitement had made Pierre's English even more broken than usual. 'Alors, but where are ze others? You got zem all out?'

'Sure, Pierre. But I can't vouch for their safety.' Dan's face lost its grin. 'I *hope* they're still aboard the telezero reflector. Dig, Sir Hubert, old Handlebars – he's an Atlantine buddy of mine. *And* Sondar!'

'Ah yes, the one good Treen.' Now it was the President speaking. 'An unusual but welcome ally, eh, Colonel?' He turned to a video screen and snapped his fingers for one of his men to report. 'Get in direct contact, Vortax. No – better. Put us alongside.'

Dan took the space-suit that the Theron President handed him and put it on. 'I'm sending a party of engineers aboard the telezero,' explained the Theron. 'You will want to lead them.'

'I appreciate that, sir.'

The two ships slid close.

It was Digby – a battle-stained and weary Digby – who met Dan as he stepped into the stricken craft. Dan couldn't keep the relief out of his voice as he greeted his batman.

'Thank the stars, Dig! What a fight you fellows put up! But what's the score?'

'Ee! Well, at close of play it were one up to us, Colonel Dan. But we've taken a proper pastin'! Sondar says the ship's well nigh unmovable!'

'Sir Hubert?'

'He's fine, sir! Fair hoppin' 'cos he couldn't go after the Treens!'

'How about the others, Dig?'

'Well, sir . . . ' Digby looked away. 'Our Atlantine chums copped it pretty bad. There's only one left . . . '

'Handlebars?' Dan was gripping his batman's arm painfully.

Digby nodded. 'Aye. Handlebars. But I'm afraid he's hurt, Colonel Dan. He – that is, even Sondar agrees with me – he won't live.'

His mind seething, Dan shouldered roughly past Digby. Now he saw him. The Dapon. Lying prone against a bulkhead, his face strained and drawn.

'Handlebars! Oh, *Handlebars!*'

The hand that clutched at him was weak. But the smile on the rugged face was serene and full of contentment. Dan choked and looked away as the Dapon laboured to force a conspiratorial wink.

'I – I settled for 'em, Dan! It wasn't in vain, my friend! Please – don't say anything. And don't tell me the truth about yourself. You *are* Kargaz – you will always be Kargaz to me!'

'Listen, old buddy. You're going to pull through. Do you hear me? You're going to pull through!' Dan was consciously exerting all his willpower to keep the fluttering thread of life going in the Atlantine non-com. 'We'll have to move you to the Theron ship.'

Now a Theron was at Dan's side. 'That's right, Colonel Dare. We will have to evacuate this vessel completely. There is no chance of taking it back to the south – but the President has ordered that samples of the armour-plating be removed for analysis. It is being done now.'

'Good,' said Dan. 'Then at least you'll be able to construct a shield against the Treens' telezero. Would you give me a hand with the Dapon here?'

'I'm tougher than I look.' Old Handlebars forced himself to his feet. There was an old glint in his eye. 'Allow an elderly soldier to walk unaided. We regulars have our pride!'

Dan smiled. 'Maybe Dig and Sondar were wrong,' he thought. 'Maybe he's going to make it after all . . . '

Meanwhile, in Mekonta, the Mekon had taken the news of his battle fleet's repulse badly. He'd forgotten himself so much that he had allowed himself a trace of the despised emotion. It was

the emotion of bleak fury!

'They must be destroyed! All of them! *Destroyed!*'

'But Mekon . . . ' The Director was gibbering in terror, at least inwardly. 'But Mekon, we cannot use the telezero against the Theron force! When you ordered maximum power to destroy the spaceport, all the built-up energy in transmitters three and seven was used up!'

'Faulty and unbrained one!' The Mekon was raving, and his aides shuddered to see this hitherto unknown side of him! 'You should have kept an adequate reserve! I condemn you to die! You and the other bunglers who have brought this reverse to Treen superiority!' The Mekon turned to the luckless Director's chief assistant. 'You. Can you send up five hundred more fighters straight away?'

'At once, Mekon!' The Treen paused. 'And such a force will at least hold the enemy occupied while the reserve telezeros are brought to full strength.'

'That is sound logic,' nodded the Mekon. 'You are hereby raised to the status of your miserable failure of a predecessor. Go now, and let there be no error!'

'What about the Earth-Plan, Mekon?'

'The Earth-Plan? *The Earth-Plan?* That can wait! *Everything* can wait! I want only the cancellation of the Theron President, his fleet, and his accursed earthling friends!'

That there was danger from Mekonta, the Theron President

was only too well aware! The samples from the telezero ship had been taken aboard, and now he hurried Dan and his friends through the entry port. 'The Treens will throw everything they have at us,' he said. 'It is vital that we get clear immediately!'

The airlocks were closed, and the President gave the order for withdrawal of his fleet. Then . . .

'Sir! Someone hasn't come aboard! Someone is going back to the Telezero ship!'

'*Whaaat?*'

A video screen clicked on, and now they could see him, stepping back into the battered giant. 'It's Handlebars!' Dan whirled round, his face ashen under its blue tinge. 'We've got to get him back!'

'No, Dan. I tell you – he's a goner anyway.' Digby laid a hand on his Colonel's arm.

'But what?'

Sondar spoke. 'The ship could not be taken to the south, Colonel Dare. But there is enough energy for it to go back to Mekonta. I think *that* is where our friend is about to deliver it!'

'Great jupiter! The fool! The crazy, gallant fool!' Dan blinked through the sight-screens of the President's command and saw the one good engine of the telezero burst into life.

'The Mekon wants his ship, does he? He wants his toy back! Then he's going to get it! Right in the neck!' The Dapon – old Handlebars – corrected the twist of the uneven drive, cork-screwing the telezero reflector through the litter of battle debris and down towards the surrounding atmosphere of Venus. He could imagine the hive of activity in Mekonta: the furious marshalling of the Treen reserve, the super-speeded re-charge of their infernally destructive machines. Yes! It was on course now. Falling – gripped by the planet's own gravity. It was on target! His eyes clouded over and the life left his body . . . but there was a smile on his soldier's face.

The concussive blast of the explosion rocked Mekonta to its foundations! The mighty ship nose-dived into the central telezero transmitter buildings and set off a sequence of pulverising chain-detonations that put north-Venusian technology a thousand years to the rear! Records, computers, laboratories – all went up in a cataclysmic holocaust whose shockwaves even rocked the old Theron capital in the south! In one suicidal second, the burgeoning flare of doom wiped out the Mekon's vaunted reserve, and his fighters were no more than a pile of blackened, twisted junk on their launch pads! With poetic justice, the sacrifice of one stalwart had rubbed out the oppression of centuries of his race's slavery ... and had ended the Venusian war!

Dan Dare – his Atlantine colour removed, sat in the Theron President's living-room. With him, his friends. *All* his friends. Sir Hubert Guest, Digby, Professor Peabody, Hank, Pierre – and Sondar.

'A report has come through,' said the President, 'that the Mekon may – I say, *may* have perished in the devastation of Mekonta. Personally, I would not be sure.'

'Aye. Like I said about Colonel Dan, I'd never believe he was gone until I was standin' by the graveside,' said Dig. 'I beg your pardon, sir!' He looked apologetically at his chief.

'But,' continued the President, 'we must take such things as truth until they are proved otherwise. And now, my friends – shall we get down to business and discuss the project by which Venus can supply fresh resources of food to the Earth?' He smiled. 'I may say that I have already given instructions for ships to be built to take the first consignment. I fancy that you would approve a reserved section for – ah – personal accommodation?'

'You mean we'll be going *with* it?' Dan laughed and looked round at his companions. 'Home's going to be paradise after this little jaunt – and even Sondar's going to find his emotions strained when he finds what a hero's welcome *he's* going to get!'

'I have no difficulty in following *that* logic, Colonel Dare,' said the Treen.